AUTUMN
PUBLISHING

Published in 2021
First published in the UK by Autumn Publishing
An imprint of Igloo Books Ltd
Cottage Farm, NN6 0BJ, UK
Owned by Bonnier Books
Sveavägen 56, Stockholm, Sweden
www.igloobooks.com

0321 001
2 4 6 8 10 9 7 5 3 1
ISBN 978-1-80022-035-5
Printed and manufactured in the UK

PROLOGUE

Long ago, before our time, there was a land called Kumandra, where humans lived alongside water dragons. The dragons brought water, rain, and peace to the land to help it flourish. And the humans lived in harmony, caring for one another. Life in Kumandra was paradise.

But then the Druun came, spreading like wildfire to consume life. Whoever they touched turned to stone. A mindless virus, the Druun cared for nothing. Their only goal was to spread and multiply.

Dragons valiantly fought the Druun, battling to save humanity, but it wasn't enough. One by one, the great and mighty dragons were turned to stone.

Until there was only one left.

When all seemed lost, Sisudatu, the last dragon, summoned every bit of her magic and power and placed it in a gem. Then she climbed to the highest point in Kumandra and brought forth a great explosion!

When the dust cleared, the Druun were gone—and so was Sisudatu.

The humans who had been turned to stone came back to life. But the dragons did not. And all that remained of Sisu was the glowing blue Dragon Gem—the last remnant of dragon magic.

Without the dragons, peace and harmony disappeared. Kumandra split into five enemy lands—Tail, Spine, Talon, Fang, and Heart—that fought to possess the Dragon Gem. It had to be hidden.

The Dragon Gem now resides in a secret chamber in Heart, guarded by the warrior Chief Benja, the baddest blade in all the lands. No one has ever gotten near the Gem . . . until now.

CHAPTER ONE

In a dark room in the Land of Heart, a young warrior readied for battle. Twelve-year-old Raya pulled on gloves. She grabbed her bamboo fighting sticks and tied a dark mask over her face. After a quick pause to pull her hair back, she slipped out into the night.

Outside, the damp night air felt charged with electricity, though whether it was from the thunderstorm or Raya's own excitement, it was hard to say. She ran lightly over the tiled rooftops of Heart Fortress. Her slippered feet hardly made a sound as she leapt, catlike, from building to building, then jumped to the ground.

The first raindrops splashed down, covering Raya's tracks as she hurried toward the Chamber of the Dragon Gem.

The fortress sat atop a natural stone arch at the center of Heart. Beneath a tangle of leaves and vines, Raya found the hidden doorway that led inside. She glanced around, making sure she was unseen, then sneaked in.

Raya crept through the torch-lit tunnel, sliding her hands along the walls. She could feel the shapes of dragons that had been carved there centuries before.

Raya paused. Something didn't feel right. There was a groove in the wall that was deeper than the carvings. . . .

She knelt and examined the damp cobblestones that lined the tunnel floor. One stone was looser than the rest. Carefully, Raya pressed it.

WHOOSH! A net dropped from the ceiling, right on the spot where she was standing. But Raya had been expecting it. She rolled backward, easily dodging the trap.

"Looks like someone's trying to be clever," Raya murmured.

Reaching into her satchel, she pulled out a small ball covered in hard scales. When she tapped it with her finger, the ball partly uncurled, revealing two bright black eyes and a cute furry face.

"All right, Tuk Tuk," Raya said to the little animal. "Let's show 'em what clever *really* looks like."

She placed her pet on the ground. Tuk Tuk curled back into a scaly ball, then rolled down the tunnel, triggering more traps. One after another, nets dropped from the ceiling. But Tuk Tuk rolled right underneath them.

Halfway through, though, Tuk Tuk spied a bug. He waddled after it, forgetting all about his job.

"Tuk Tuk!" Raya whispered. "Come on. Focus."

Tuk Tuk curled back into a ball and rolled to the end of the tunnel.

Raya crawled under the nets to where he was waiting. She gently picked Tuk Tuk up and patted his head. "Hey, bud. That was awesome. Gimme some shell."

Tuk Tuk tried to high-five her, but he lost his balance and rolled onto his back.

"I gotcha." Raya turned him upright, then placed him back in her satchel.

Ahead of her was a large circular stone door. Raya removed her fighting sticks from her belt and unlocked it. Wiggling out of her shoes and leaving them at the entrance, Raya stepped through the opening. She gasped in wonder. Incandescent blue flowers dotted the darkness like stars, lighting the way. Emerald water flowed against gravity up a flight of stone steps. She was entering the Chamber of the Dragon Gem.

Four great dragon statues held up the ceiling, which was open to the sky. The floor was a pond. And in the center of the chamber, suspended in midair by its own magic, was the glowing Dragon Gem.

Raya took a deep breath. This was it—the moment she'd prepared for all her life.

A series of stepping-stones led over the water to the center of the room. Raya started across them, then paused. "Wait a second . . . this feels too easy."

She turned and glanced behind her. When she looked forward again, she saw a golden-masked warrior standing between her and the Gem.

Raya's grip tightened on her fighting sticks. "Chief Benja, look, I know it's your job to try to stop me, but you won't," she said.

"Don't mistake spirit for skill, young one," the chief replied. Behind the golden mask, his voice sounded deep. Raya glanced at the sword at his waist. Chief Benja's sword was well-known to Raya. Its curved blade could expand into a whip that would take out three warriors at once. It wasn't skill alone that made Chief Benja the baddest blade in the lands.

"You might want to take out that blade," Raya said boldly, though her heart was pounding. "You're going to need it."

"Not today." Chief Benja detached his sword from his belt, but he didn't unsheathe it.

In a quick move, Raya lunged to the left, hoping to catch the warrior off guard. Chief Benja blocked her path. Raya's fighting sticks spun through the air. But each time, they missed.

When she saw an opening, Raya tried to dodge the chief, her feet searching for purchase on the slippery rocks. For a moment, it seemed like she might slip past.

With a swift parry, Chief Benja disarmed her and knocked her down. Her fighting sticks clattered on the stones.

Raya sprawled on the ground, struggling to catch her breath. Chief Benja stood over her. For a long second, they stared at each other. Then, with the tip of his sheathed sword, he reached out and tapped Raya's nose. "Boop."

He lifted his golden mask. Raya looked up into her father's face. His eyes were full of pride as he smiled down at her.

"Like I said, not one foot in the inner circle. You lost, Raya," he said.

Raya raised one eyebrow. "Did I?"

Her father glanced down. Raya's foot was stretched out in front her. The tip of her toe rested on the Dragon Gem's inner circle.

"Raya . . ." Her father shook his head and chuckled. "I probably should have said *two* feet."

Raya stood up, grinning. "Hey. Don't beat yourself up too much, Chief Benja. You gave it your best."

"I won't. And it's either Father or Ba to you. You did

good, dewdrop," he said, using the old Kumandran term of endearment. "You passed the test."

He held out a hand to Raya, inviting her to join him in the inner circle.

Raya paused, savoring the moment. Her dream, at last, had come true. She stepped into the inner circle.

The Dragon Gem hovered just inches away, washing her face in blue light. Up close, Raya could see the glimmer within the stone. She could feel the power of its magic.

"Wow," she whispered. "The spirit of Sisu."

Benja knelt and bowed, raising his hands in a circle before his forehead. Raya did the same. She watched, entranced, as tiny droplets of water rose into the air, swirling and spiraling around the Gem.

"For generations, our family has sworn to protect the Gem," Benja told his daughter. "Today, you will join that legacy."

Benja scooped up a handful of the sacred water and poured it over Raya's bowed head. As the water trickled over Raya's face, the droplets began to glow. They floated away from her to join the drops encircling the Gem.

"Raya, Princess of Heart, my daughter," Benja intoned. "You are now a Guardian of the Dragon Gem."

Benja wrapped his arm proudly around his daughter. She leaned her head against his shoulder, at once exhausted and elated. For as long as Raya could remember, she had worked for this rite of passage to guardianship. All the months and years of training had been worth it. This was everything she'd ever wanted.

CHAPTER TWO

The sun was just starting to rise as Raya and her father left the Chamber of the Dragon Gem. The sound of chickens clucking filled the early-morning air, which felt cool against Raya's skin.

Heart sat in the center of the dragon-shaped Kumandran River, right where the dragon's heart would have been. Fed by water from the great river, the Land of Heart was lush and green.

Inside the palace, Raya led the way down the halls. She walked a few paces ahead of her father, throwing strokes and kicks as she went.

Her father watched with amusement. "Well, someone's excited," he said.

"Well, yeah," she said. "I mean, anyone hoping to steal

the Dragon Gem now has to face the fury of the *two* baddest blades in all the lands."

"Well, I'm glad you feel prepared, dewdrop," Benja said, "because I have something important to tell you. The other lands? They're on their way here as we speak."

Raya whirled around. "They are?" Watching her father nod, she continued, "Okay, *okay,* we can do this. I'm ready. I know exactly how we'll stop them."

"Really? Tell me what you know about the other lands," he said.

Raya's imagination took her to a desert region where a mercenary was sharpening and slashing his blade. She could see it as clearly as if it was before her eyes. "First, Tail. A sweltering desert with sneaky mercenaries who fight dirty."

Next, she imagined a port city where a merchant tossed fruit into the air, slicing it with a pair of knives as it fell. "Second, Talon. A floating market famous for fast deals and fighters with even faster hands."

On to snow-covered mountains that were home to an army of barbarians. "Third, Spine. A frigid bamboo forest guarded by exceptionally large warriors and their giant axes," Raya explained to her father.

Last but not least were the warriors of Fang. Raya imagined them holding big cats in their arms. "Fourth, Fang, our fiercest enemy. A nation protected by angry assassins and their even angrier cats. Hiss!"

Tuk Tuk hissed, too, as they entered the palace kitchen.

"Okay, so we're gonna need crossbows. And catapults. Ooh, what about flaming catapults?" she said.

Benja added ingredients into a simmering pot. "Or . . . how about shrimp paste from Tail, lemongrass from Talon, bamboo shoots from Spine, chilies from Fang, and palm sugar from Heart?"

"We'll poison them?" she asked.

"No, we're not going to poison them, and we're not going to fight them. We're going to share a meal with them," Benja said as he handed her a bowl of soup.

"Wait. What?" Raya stared at her father.

"I invited them."

"But they're our enemies," Raya said, confused.

"They're only our enemies because they think the Dragon Gem magically brings us prosperity," he said.

Raya scoffed. "That's ridiculous. It doesn't do that."

"They assume it does, just like we assume things about them," Benja said. "Raya, there's a reason why each land is named after a part of the dragon. We were once unified harmoniously as one: Kumandra."

"That's ancient history, Ba," she said, sipping the soup.

"But it doesn't have to be. Listen, if we don't stop and

learn to trust one another again, it's only a matter of time before we tear each other apart. This isn't the world I want you to live in."

Raya sighed.

"I believe that we can be Kumandra again, but someone has to take the first step. Trust me."

Raya looked at her father. She *did* trust him. Chief Benja had never steered Heart wrong. Surely he knew what he was doing.

CHAPTER THREE

The next day, the chiefs of Tail, Talon, Spine, and Fang arrived in Heart. Raya accompanied her father to welcome them. Dressed in blue and gold silk, the two stood side by side on the bridge that connected Heart to the mainland. Together, they looked out at a crowd.

For the chiefs had not come alone. Each had arrived with an army of warriors. The clans stood apart from one another, identified by pennants bearing the symbols of their lands. But Raya hardly noticed the colorful flags. She was focused on the swords and spears that bristled from the crowd.

"Things look a little tense, Ba," Raya whispered to her father.

"Don't worry. I'm gonna open with a joke," he whispered back.

Raya rolled her eyes. "Please don't."

"I'm kidding, I'm kidding," he said. Then he stepped forward and held out his arms in greeting. Raising his voice to be heard by all, he called out, "People of Tail, Talon, Spine, and Fang, welcome to Heart. For far too long we have been enemies. But today is a new day. Today, we can be Kumandra once more."

Smiling warmly, he stepped aside, inviting the other clans to cross the bridge and enter Heart.

No one moved. The chiefs regarded Benja with narrowed eyes, their faces etched with suspicion.

"Nice speech, Chief Benja," growled the chief of Tail. She was a small woman dressed in earth-colored clothes. "But why did you really bring us here? Are you going to rob us?"

"Why would he need to rob us? The Land of Heart already has everything," snarled an imposing man wearing vibrant purple robes. It was Dang Hai, the fierce-looking chief of Talon.

"It's easy to pontificate on Kumandra when you hold the mightiest weapon in all the lands," shouted the chief of Spine, a burly warrior dressed in furs.

"The Gem's not a weapon—it's a sacred relic," Chief Benja replied.

A chorus of angry voices filled the air as the leaders began to shout over one another.

Raya looked around. This was not going as her father had

planned. She noticed a girl her age, the only other kid there. As their eyes met, they shared a smile.

Raya stepped forward, bowed respectfully to the clans, and said, "I have something to say . . ."

Silence fell over the crowd.

She continued, "Who's hungry?"

A lone hand went up. It belonged to a warrior from Spine. But he quickly lowered it when his fellow warriors shot him disapproving looks.

The other girl giggled at him. She looked up at her mother, Virana, the chief of Fang.

"Go ahead. It's all right," said Virana.

The Fang princess walked over to Raya. Like her mother, she was dressed in white silk. Her short black hair fell like a curtain over half her face; the other side of her head was shaved.

"I'm Namaari. Of Fang," she said.

"Hi, Namaari. I'm Raya." She noticed Namaari was wearing a necklace with a dragon-shaped pendant. "Is that Sisu?" Raya asked, pointing at it. Then she caught herself. "Sorry. Um, yeah, I might be a little bit of a dragon nerd."

Namaari smiled. "Hey, I'm the one wearing the Sisu fan necklace."

Raya returned the smile. Right then, she decided she liked the princess. "Come on. Have you eaten yet?"

Side by side, the new friends walked across the bridge. Watching them, Chief Benja smiled with pride.

The sight of the two girls together seemed to pacify the other grown-ups. At a sign from the chiefs, the warriors lowered their swords. The clans followed their leaders across the bridge into Heart.

Awaiting them was a celebration like none Raya had ever seen. The great hall of Heart Palace had been decorated with fresh flowers and silk curtains. The tables were piled high with rice cakes, dumplings, spring rolls, buns, fruit, and other good things to eat. A band played lively music. Yet for all the festive trappings, the atmosphere was tense. The chiefs stood apart, eyeing one another suspiciously.

Only Raya and Namaari were having fun. They sat at the edge of the room with Tuk Tuk, each holding a tray of snacks.

"Seriously? Your mom actually said that? Awkward. Okay, next question: hand-to-hand or swords?" Raya asked.

"Blades all day," answered Namaari.

"Right?" Raya said, giving Namaari the Kumandran fist bump.

It was Namaari's turn to ask a question. "Okay . . . dressy or casual?"

"Only a monster would choose to wear this outfit on the regular. Rice or stew?" To Raya's surprise, Namaari hesitated. "I didn't think that'd stump you."

"This is actually one of the first times I've had rice in a while," Namaari admitted.

"Really?" Raya asked.

"Fang may look nice on the outside," Namaari explained. "But we have some pretty big holes on the inside."

"Oh." Raya didn't know what to say.

"Sorry, didn't mean to bring it down," Namaari said quickly, flashing a smile. "So where were we? We both have single parents who are terrible at telling jokes, we're both warrior women who despise uncomfortable formal wear—"

"*And* we're both Sisu superfans."

Namaari lowered her voice. "You know, Fang legend says she's still out there."

"Sisu? You're kidding, right?" Raya said.

Namaari glanced around to make sure no one was looking. "Hey, want to see something?" From a fold in her tunic, she withdrew an ancient manuscript. Raya could tell from the way Namaari held it that it was very old and very special.

"Are you supposed to have that?" Raya whispered.

Namaari laughed. "No," she said, as if it was obvious. Carefully, she unfolded the fragile palm leaves that made up the manuscript.

It was covered with an intricate design. Raya could tell it was a scene depicting Sisu and the Druun.

"According to this, after the mighty Sisu blasted away all the Druun, she fell into the water and floated downstream," Namaari explained. "Legends say she's now sleeping at the river's end."

Tuk Tuk wandered over to sniff the manuscript. Raya patted his shell absently. "But which river?" she asked. "There's, like, hundreds."

"I don't know," Namaari admitted. "But if we could find it, could you imagine? A dragon back in the world? Things could be so much better."

Raya glanced at her father. "Yeah, maybe we really could be Kumandra again."

"Here," Namaari said. She took off her dragon necklace and held it out to Raya.

"Whoa. Really?" Raya asked, accepting the gift.

"From one dragon nerd to another."

Raya looked at the dragon pendant and back at Namaari. Her father said she needed to trust. And she trusted Namaari. Suddenly, she knew what to do.

"Hey, come with me, dep la," Raya said, using the

Kumandran phrase for *best friend*. "I want to show you something." She stood, brushing a few grains of rice from her tunic.

Namaari gave her a curious look, then stood, too.

Unnoticed by any of the grown-ups, they stole from the palace. Tuk Tuk snatched a quick bite of food, then scurried after them.

CHAPTER FOUR

Raya led Namaari down the long tunnel to the Chamber of the Dragon Gem, the same one Raya had passed through in her initiation the day before. This time, there were no nets to slow them down. As an official Guardian, Raya now knew how to deactivate the traps. Within moments, they reached the circular door.

At the entrance to the inner chamber, the girls slipped off their shoes, and Raya led the way up the stairs. When Namaari stepped into the great chamber and saw the Dragon Gem, her eyes widened.

"The spirit of Sisu. I can feel it." Namaari's voice was full of awe. She bowed and formed her hands in a circle in front of her head.

Raya smiled. She knew just how Namaari felt. "It's the last bit of dragon magic left in the whole world."

"I can see why Heart guards it so closely. Thank you, *dep la*. You've been very helpful," Namaari said in a cold voice.

A hard blow landed in the middle of Raya's spine as Namaari kicked her to the ground. Raya looked up at her new friend in shock. Her mind struggled to make sense of what was happening.

"In a different world, maybe we could have been friends. But I have to do what's right for Fang," Namaari snarled down at her. The sweet, shy girl she'd been only moments before had vanished.

Namaari started toward the Dragon Gem. But Raya had not trained as a warrior for nothing. Scrambling to her feet, she leapt in front of Namaari, blocking her path.

Namaari swung at her with a swift strike. Raya dodged the blow and countered it. But Namaari was fierce. She came hard at Raya, raining kicks and blows. With dawning alarm, Raya realized that Namaari was a skilled fighter. She wasn't sure how long she could hold her off.

Seeing Raya in trouble, Tuk Tuk tried to help. Tucking himself into a ball, he rolled hard and bumped against Namaari's ankle. Namaari scooted him away.

But the second of distraction was just enough. Raya aimed a kick that caught Namaari off guard, knocking her down.

To her surprise, Namaari smiled. She pulled a firework from the folds of her clothes and lit it. The rocket shot through the open roof of the chamber and burst into a bright red flower overhead.

Back at the palace, Benja had finally begun making some headway with the other chiefs. He was talking to Chief Virana, the leader of Fang, when the firework exploded.

Benja stared up at it in wonder. Fireworks? That hadn't been part of the planned celebration.

There was a shuffling around them. The Fang soldiers were moving toward the door. Benja glanced out the window. Warriors carrying lit torches were climbing the path to the chamber. From their white clothing, Benja could tell they were from Fang.

Benja turned to Chief Virana for an explanation. But she was gone.

In the Chamber of the Dragon Gem, Raya and Namaari were still locked in combat.

"There's no way you're taking Sisu's gem," Raya snarled, aiming a kick at Namaari's ribs.

"Sorry. It's Fang's now," Namaari shot back, striking Raya's head.

At that moment, an army of Fang warriors spilled into the room. They formed a protective circle around Namaari.

Raya stepped back. For the first time since their fight had started, she felt a stab of real fear. The Fang warriors far outnumbered her.

But she was the only thing standing between Fang and the Dragon Gem. It was her duty to protect the Gem no matter what.

Raya squared her shoulders, readying herself for the fight, until—

SWOOSH! A dark figure rappelled down through the chamber's open roof. Raya's heart lifted. It was her father!

Chief Benja landed next to Raya on a stone platform beneath the Gem. The Fang soldiers surged forward. But Benja blocked their way. His sword became a whip, and it drove back one Fang soldier after another.

"You will not set foot on the Dragon Gem's inner circle," he declared.

Raya smiled. Her father was definitely the baddest blade in all of Kumandra.

But then, a loud voice rang out. "What's going on?" The warriors from Spine had entered the room.

The chief of Spine eyed the Fang soldiers. "What is this?"

But the Spine army wasn't alone. A moment later, the armies from Tail and Talon shuffled into the room. They all stared at the Dragon Gem, awed by its power.

"Fang's making a play for the Gem!" the Spine warrior exclaimed.

"No! Spine should have the Gem!" the chief of Spine cried.

"Not if we get to it first!" shouted the chief of Tail.

Raya watched in horror as warriors from each army raised their weapons. If she and her father didn't do something, there was going to be a bloodbath!

Chief Benja had his sword raised, too. But to Raya's alarm, he suddenly lowered it. "Listen to me!" he cried. "We have a choice. We can tear each other apart, or we come together and build a better world. It's not too late. I still believe we can be Kumandra again. . . ."

As the astonished warriors watched, Chief Benja sheathed his sword.

For a long moment, no one moved. Raya could hardly breathe. Her father had taken a great gamble. Would it pay off?

Out of the corner of her eye, Raya saw a slight movement. A Fang soldier at the back of the crowd raised his crossbow and fired.

With a soft *fffft*, the arrow sliced through the air and struck Chief Benja in the leg. He sank to the ground, crying out in pain.

"Ba!" Raya screamed. For a second she forgot about the Gem as she ran to help him.

Gritting his teeth, Benja pulled the arrow from his leg. The other chiefs saw their chance. At once, they all rushed toward the Dragon Gem, clawing past one another to grab it. The Gem flew from hand to hand as they snatched and pummeled each other to gain hold.

"Give me the Gem!"

"Out of my way!"

"The Gem belongs to Spine!"

CRASH!

The Gem hit the ground, breaking into five pieces.

BOOM! An earthquake shook the room. The water in the chamber began to recede. A crack split the stone floor open, and darkness emerged. Black as night, with a purple shine, it whirled toward the horrified crowd.

"Druun . . ." Benja gasped. For the first time in her life, Raya saw her father look truly afraid.

A warrior fired an arrow at the creature, but it passed right through. A second later, the Druun had turned the warrior to stone and duplicated itself.

The darkness now turned toward Benja and Raya. Benja quickly grabbed one of the glowing Gem pieces and held it aloft. The Druun shrank back, repelled by the powerful magic.

"There's still magic in them! Get the pieces!" one of the chiefs cried.

"No!" shouted Raya.

There was another crazed scramble as the chiefs snatched up the four remaining Gem fragments.

"Ba! Come on! We have to go!" Raya grabbed her father's sword. She put her shoulders under his arm and pulled him from the room. Benja leaned hard on her. The ground rolled and shook beneath their feet, and clouds of dust rained around them as they hurried away from the chamber. A Druun pursued them, but when it came in contact with the remaining water, it recoiled.

Chief Benja saw this happen. "They're repelled by water!" he said to himself. Then, to whoever could hear him, he shouted, "Hurry! Get to the river!"

Raya led her father and Tuk Tuk toward the Heart Bridge, but she couldn't go fast enough. The sword was heavy, and Benja was heavier. He was badly hurt and could only limp along, leaning most of his weight on Raya's slim shoulders. All around, terrified people shoved past them, running for their lives.

Halfway across the long bridge, Benja's leg gave out. He fell to the ground, dragging Raya with him.

At once she was up again, trying with all her might to

pull him back onto his feet. "Ba! Get up!" she screamed. "Come on. Please, we have to keep moving. Get up."

Beneath them the ground began to shake. A Druun moved onto the bridge.

"Please, Ba!" Raya cried desperately, redoubling her efforts. "We don't have time. Look. Stand up! I'll help you."

Benja looked at her sadly. "Raya, you have to listen. You are the Guardian of the Dragon Gem."

"Ba, why are you saying this?" Raya asked in alarm.

Her father pulled out the broken Gem shard. "There's still light in this. There's still hope."

Raya realized what he meant. He wanted her to go on—without him. Her heart nearly broke in two. "No, we can make it together," she insisted. "You're okay. . . ."

Benja placed the Gem shard in Raya's hand, wrapping her fingers tightly around it. "Raya, don't give up on them." He pulled her close and kissed her forehead. "I love you, my dewdrop."

Raya didn't want to leave him. "Ba? No!"

The words had barely left her lips when her father pushed her over the side of the bridge. As she fell toward the water, along with Tuk Tuk and the sword, Raya saw the Druun pass through her father, turning him to stone.

"No!" Raya shouted.

Splash! She hit the water hard and surfaced with a gasp.

Waves slapped at her face. Paddling frantically, she looked up at the still stone figure of her father.

"Ba!" Raya screamed as the current carried her away.

CHAPTER FIVE

The years that followed were the hardest Raya had ever known. After the day that Namaari ruined her life, as she thought of it, Raya never returned to Heart. She told herself there was no point in going back. Without her father or the Dragon Gem, there was nothing there for her. But the truth was she couldn't bring herself to cross the Heart Bridge. Her last glimpse of her father there, frozen in stone, still haunted her.

From that day on, Raya began a quest that took her all over Kumandra. Ironically, it was Namaari who'd given her the idea. That day at the banquet, Namaari had shown her the ancient manuscript that said Sisudatu, the last dragon, slept at the end of a riverbed. If Raya could find the right river, maybe she could wake Sisu. Then the dragon could blast the Druun away again and bring back her ba.

Raya knew it was a desperate plan. But it was her only hope, and she clung to it.

Weeks stretched into months, and months stretched into years as Raya traveled from Heart to Talon to Spine to Fang, following every river to its end. She knelt before hundreds of streams, praying to Sisu for help. Each time the dragon failed to appear, Raya's heart broke a little more. But she refused to give up. Without this single hope, she had nothing left at all.

Six years after she started her quest, Raya arrived in Tail, the furthest region of the land that had once been Kumandra. She'd been only a girl when she left Heart. Now she was a tall young woman with black hair that flowed out from under a hat shaped like a Kumandran temple. Her skin was darkened from the sun. Her arms had grown strong from wielding her father's sword, which she carried with her always.

Tuk Tuk had grown bigger, too—much, *much* bigger. The roly-poly critter was now the size of a horse. When curled into a ball, he rolled at an astonishing speed. With Tuk Tuk's help, Raya was able to travel much faster than she could have on foot.

Tail was a vast desert of sand and rock. Sitting astride a rolling Tuk Tuk, Raya raced through it. They left a plume of dust in their wake.

As Raya took in the strange tall rock formations, she wondered if she'd made a mistake. There was hardly any water here. It seemed an unlikely place to find a water creature like Sisudatu.

Still, Raya had vowed to visit every river in Kumandra. And there was still one river she hadn't searched.

Suddenly, on the dusty horizon, she spotted four silhouettes. Raya put her hand on the hilt of her father's sword. Namaari had taught her a lesson she'd never forgotten—trust no one. Her years of travel through the lands of Heart's enemies had only reinforced it.

But as she drew nearer, Raya saw that the figures were made of stone. Four more people lost to the Druun.

Raya slowed, peering at the figures as she passed. Three tall and one short. A family, Raya guessed. The statues were standing next to an overturned cart. From the look of it, they'd been traveling when they were overtaken by Druun. For some reason, the Druun left their victims standing with their heads bowed, their hands cupped as if in supplication. In her years of travel, Raya had seen hundreds of stone figures. They never failed to send a shiver down her spine.

She came to a stop further on, pulled her mask down, and knocked a few times on Tuk Tuk's shell to get him to unfurl. She pulled the ancient manuscript from her saddlebag and unfolded it. The image on the manuscript was like a map, and it was covered with Xs—one for each river she'd searched. Now, finally, she'd come to the last one.

Raya lowered the manuscript and looked down at the canyon below her. It could hardly be called a river. A thin ribbon of water meandered through the nearly dry riverbed that led to a shipwreck. Still, according to the manuscript, this was the place.

She sighed. "Please let this be it."

Raya felt Tuk Tuk start to wander sideways. Looking down, she saw he was curiously following a lizard.

She rapped on his shell. "Whoa, what are you doing, you big fur bug? Hey, buddy, focus. Eyes forward, Tuk Tuk."

Finally, she succeeded in turning Tuk Tuk back toward the canyon.

"Good boy," Raya said, giving him a pat. "You're so easily distracted—"

A Druun suddenly burst from a crack in the ground in front of them. Tuk Tuk reared, and Raya tumbled from his back.

As the Druun spun toward them, Raya lunged for her satchel. She pulled out the Gem piece her father had given her and raised it into the air a second before the Druun reached her. The Druun shrank back, then disappeared into the earth.

Raya lowered the Gem shard, breathing hard. Her heart thundered in her chest. Druun were everywhere, especially in places like Tail, where there was little water. But she never got used to them.

Raya turned and saw that Tuk Tuk had rolled onto his back. His feet stuck up helplessly in the air.

"You're getting a little too big for this, bud," Raya said, grunting as she turned him back over.

Down in the canyon, Raya and Tuk Tuk followed the narrow stream until they came to a rock wall. The shipwreck was collapsed against it like the remains of some ancient beast, its wood as dry and sun-bleached as a pile of old bones. The trickle of water disappeared inside.

"Six years of searching, and we end up at a literal shipwreck," Raya observed. "That's not a bad sign, is it?"

She climbed down from Tuk Tuk's back and started toward a hole in the hull of the ship. Tuk Tuk tried to follow, but he was too big to fit through the narrow opening.

Taking a deep breath, she ducked down and crawled inside.

The little stream flowed right through the wreckage. Raya followed it past splintered boards and collapsed rigging, until she came to a sheer wall of rocks. Raya looked for another passage, but there was no way through.

This was it. She'd reached the river's end.

Raya removed her boots and hat. From her satchel, she took out a bowl and filled it with some food. She unfolded a painting of Sisu fighting the Druun and laid it down, then lit a candle. She grabbed the dragon pendant next, holding it tightly as she started to speak.

"Sisudatu . . . I don't know if you're listening. I've searched every river to find you. And now I'm here at the very last one. Look, there's not a lot of us left, and we really . . . we really need your help. If I can be honest, *I* really need your help. I made a mistake. I trusted someone I shouldn't have. And now the world's broken." Raya paused. "Sisudatu, I just really . . . really want my ba back. Please."

Raya wiped her tears away and took a deep breath. "Okay. Here goes everything," she said to herself. Then she raised a vial of water to her head and bowed. She poured the water over the pendant in the bowl and began a chant that respectfully called on the majestic dragon, creator of the Gem, to please return.

"Suva de dra sim. Mandra de dra lim. Bavaa de dra tomben."

Raya poured the last of the water and raised the vial to her head again.

Then she waited.

In the silence, Raya hung her head, too crushed to move. Six long years of searching.

And it had all come to nothing.

Raya turned. Something seemed wrong. That's when she noticed the stream. It was flowing *backward*. Then water droplets were rising into the air and swirling.

Tuk Tuk, still at the entrance, could see all that was happening. He started barking to get Raya's attention.

She turned to him. "I know, buddy, I haven't forgot—"

Then she noticed something amazing. The water droplets were joining together and forming a great cloud. Deep within the cloud, something was taking shape. It had a serpentine body and long tail, and on its head was a crest.

"Where am I?" said a raspy voice. "Pengu? Amba? Pranee? Are ya here?"

"Oh mighty Sisu," Raya said, bowing deeply.

"Who said that?" The dragon swung around, knocking Raya over with her tail.

As the dragon looked around, Raya gaped in wonder. Though she'd been dreaming of this moment for years, she was still unprepared to see a real live dragon.

The dragon had a sinuous body covered in blue-green fur and a long tail that ended in fins. A silvery, iridescent mane framed her face, and her purple eyes were bright with curiosity. Atop her head was a crest that rose like a flame. Raya would have recognized her anywhere.

"Hello? Hello?" Sisu continued.

Raya tried to respond, but she was stuck under the dragon.

Sisu realized her mistake. "Ooh, I'm sorry," she rasped. "I didn't see ya there." She picked Raya up by one leg and dusted her off. "Not too bad. Just a little dusty. Let me get that for you."

"Sisu. You are . . . Sisu!" Raya exclaimed.

"And you're . . . people. What's your name?" Sisu said.

"Raya. I'm Raya."

"And you're *not* made of stone, which means . . ."

"It worked!" They both squealed in unison.

"We did it! Ya hear that, Pengu? It worked! I didn't mess it up!" Sisu continued. Then her eyes fell on the food offering. She dropped Raya. "Is that food? I was so focused on saving the world, I forgot to have breakfast today."

Raya sat up. "Today? When exactly do you think *today* is?"

"Tuesday." Sisu took a bite of the food. "Ugh! I mean . . . *mmmm*. What is this delightful culinary treat?"

"It's jackfruit jerky," Raya replied. "I dried it myself."

"Well, compliments to the chef. Wanna finish this, skippy?" Sisu held out the jerky to Tuk Tuk, but he turned up his nose.

"Uh, Sisu, there are a few things I need to catch you up on," Raya said carefully.

"Oh yeah?" Sisu said.

With a sinking heart, Raya filled her in and held out the Gem. Or what was left of it.

"You broke it?!" Sisu hollered. "Oh, oh, oh my." She started to pace, shaking her head. "Oh, this is bad. This is bad. I've been asleep for five hundred years, you brought back the Druun, and none of my brothers and sisters came back? Why didn't they come back?"

"I . . . don't know," Raya said.

"Also, you broke the Gem."

"We still have a big chunk of it, though," Raya said hopefully.

"Is that supposed to make me feel better?" Sisu exclaimed. "If you lost a puppy, and I said, 'Well, we still have a big chunk of it,' would that make you feel better?"

"Can you just make another one?" Raya asked.

"No, I can't just *make another one,*" Sisu snapped.

"But you're a dragon," said Raya.

Sisu faced her. "I'm gonna be real with you, all right? I'm not, like, the *best* dragon. You know?"

"But you saved the world," Raya said.

"I did do that. That's true. But . . ." Sisu hesitated, trying to find the right words. "Have you ever done a group project, and there's that one kid who didn't pitch in as much but still ended up with the same grade? Yeah . . . I wasn't the one who actually made the Gem. I just . . . turned it in."

Sisu reached over and picked up the Gem fragment. The moment it touched her claws, her body began to glow with a soft blue light.

Raya stared. "Whoa, you're glowing!"

"Oh, thank you," Sisu replied with a modest wave of her hand. "I use aloe and river slime to maintain my—"

"No, no. Look." Raya pointed to Sisu's tail. In the dimness of the wreck, it shone like a lantern.

Sisu gasped. She twisted this way and that, admiring herself. "This was my little sister Amba's magic. I got the glow!"

"Your little sister's magic?" Raya asked.

"Yeah, every dragon has a unique magic."

"Okay. What's yours?"

"I'm a really strong swimmer!"

Raya's mind was spinning. Maybe there *was* something they could do. "Wait, wait. You touched this Gem piece, and it gave you powers. You know what that means, right?"

"I no longer need a night-light?" Sisu guessed.

"What? No, you're still connected to the Gem's magic. And that means you can still use it to save the world—if we get all the other Gem pieces," Raya explained.

Together, they realized that Sisu could do two important things: reassemble the Dragon Gem and blast the Druun away!

"And bring my ba back?" Raya asked, hardly daring to hope.

"And bring *all* of Kumandra back," Sisu said, beaming.

CHAPTER SIX

Not far away, a band of Fang soldiers charged through the desert. They were riding Serlots, giant cats native to Fang. As they passed the spot where the Druun had attacked Raya and Tuk Tuk, one soldier paused and turned back. She reached down to pluck a hairpin from the dusty ground.

The soldier was Namaari. Like Raya, she was older, taller, and stronger. But her hair was still shaved short on one side. As she examined the hairpin, her eyes were shrewd and calculating.

A soldier named Wahn stepped up to her. "Princess Namaari, the Tail lands are infested with Druun. Benja's daughter is as good as stone out here. Retrieving some useless ancient manuscript isn't worth the risk."

Namaari glanced at him coolly. Without warning, she struck him. He collapsed on the ground.

She looked around at the other soldiers. "Anyone else want to question why we're out here?"

The soldiers remained silent, staring at their felled comrade. Climbing back onto her Serlot, Namaari led them forward, following Tuk Tuk's tracks all the way to the shipwreck.

The soldiers dismounted and drew their weapons. Silently, they crept toward the wreck.

But when they looked inside, it was empty. Raya was already gone.

Their first stop, Raya decided, would be the Tail ruins. Raya had seen the crumbling sandstone temple as she passed through Tail. It seemed the most likely place for the Tail chief and her Gem shard to be hiding.

As they raced through the desert on Tuk Tuk's back, Raya caught Sisu up on her plan.

"Okay, so here's the sitch. After the Gem broke, each piece was taken by one of the chiefs of the five lands—Fang, Heart, Spine, Talon, and Tail, where we are now."

They arrived at the ruins. The great sandstone fortress rose up before them, silent as a tomb.

As Raya climbed off Tuk Tuk's back, she stared up at the

tall rock walls. Symbols of the five lands of Kumandra had been carved into the stone.

"Wow, so many questions," Sisu said. "First one—why am I wearing this?" She gestured to her outfit. Raya had disguised Sisu in a broad hat and long traveling cloak.

"Well, we don't want to attract attention," Raya explained.

"Oh, you definitely chose the right hat for that," Sisu said as she hopped down from Tuk Tuk and started forward. "So what makes you think the Tail chief's here?"

The words were hardly out of Sisu's mouth when her foot brushed against a wire no wider than a hair.

A tree trunk covered in metal spikes toppled, crashing toward the spot where Sisu was standing. Raya dove and pushed her out of the way in the nick of time. She got to her feet, dusting herself off. "Because I don't think this place just booby-trapped itself," she replied.

Leaving Tuk Tuk outside, Raya and Sisu entered the temple. Inside, they had to move slowly, stepping carefully over trip wires that crisscrossed the corridors. Raya was certain now they'd found the home of Tail's Gem shard. She'd never seen so many traps in one place.

"This doesn't make sense," Sisu said. "None of this would stop a Druun."

"It's not to stop Druun. It's to stop people," Raya explained.

"Hmm," Sisu murmured.

They arrived at a hallway that was filled with an intricate array of trip wires. While Raya again carefully worked her way through it, Sisu quickly and smoothly flew through it without a single problem, ending with a smile. Raya watched in astonishment.

"What? Why are you looking at me like that?" Sisu asked.

Raya smiled. "Uh . . . nothing. Just not used to seeing dragons."

"Impressed, huh? Wait till you see my backstroke. I'm wicked when I hit that liquid. I got water skills that kill. I slaughter when I hit the water. I'm like . . . really good at swimming. Through rhyme. I was trying to make . . . that I was a really good swimmer . . . I'm a good swimmer is basically what I'm saying. . . ." Sisu trailed off.

"Okay. We need to keep moving," Raya said.

They soon rounded another dark corner.

"Oh no!" Sisu cried suddenly.

Raya nearly jumped out of her boots. She spun around, drawing her sword. But she couldn't see any danger. "What? What is it?"

"We forgot to bring a gift for the Tail chief," said the dragon. She seemed truly upset.

Raya looked at her blankly. "I'm sorry, a gift?"

"Yeah. A gift says 'You can trust me, can I trust you?'" Sisu explained.

A shiny beetle flew down and landed on Sisu's nose. "Aw, hey there, little fella!" She held it up to the light and laughed as the beetle raised its bottom in the air. "Oh, this beetle's got a booty!"

When Raya saw what Sisu was holding, she froze. "Careful! It's a toot-and-boom!"

"Why is it called a—"

But before Sisu could finish, the beetle suddenly spread its wings and rose into the air. Raya tackled Sisu as it exploded.

"Got it," said Sisu. "Noted. Makes sense."

Raya didn't respond. She was peering into a narrow tunnel ahead. By the light of the torch, they could see the walls were covered in beetles.

"You have to admit, though, these bug booties are kinda cute," Sisu said.

Holding their breath, Raya and Sisu crept through the tunnel, being careful not to disturb the insects. Raya could hear the bugs crawling on top of each other. The clicking sound of their legs caused the hairs on her neck to stand on end. But she and Sisu made it through the passage without an explosion.

They entered a vast cavern. A deep chasm separated

them from a natural rock platform. A dead tree stood in the middle of the rock, its bare branches twisted like claws. Curled in the hollow of the tree was a skeleton, the Dragon Gem shard clasped tight in its bony fingers. Raya and Sisu silently took in the grisly sight.

"I'd say we found the Tail chief," Raya said at last.

"What happened to her?" Sisu murmured.

"From the looks of it, she was hoarding the Gem and became a victim of her own traps," Raya replied.

"Well, you got to admire her commitment," Sisu said.

They looked around for a way across, but the bridge was long gone. They needed another way to get onto the platform.

"Okay. Hold on," Raya told Sisu.

Sisu grabbed Raya's shoulders as Raya used her grappling sword to swing them across the chasm.

But halfway across, they stopped in midair. Raya glanced back and saw that Sisu was still clinging to the ledge with her hind feet.

"Oh." Sisu looked embarrassed. "We were doing a jumpy thing. So sorry. My bad. I get it now. I'm with it."

Sisu jumped, carrying Raya with her. They landed easily on the other side, where Sisu reached for the Gem shard.

"Sisu? Don't," Raya said.

Sisu froze. Raya pointed to the thin wire connected to the skeleton's hand. She traced the wire's path up and across the ceiling, where it ended in a trapdoor above the entrance to the cavern.

Raya studied the trap. The wire was tied to the same hand that held the Gem shard. Removing the shard would cause the skeleton's hand to raise. She had to figure out a way to take it without tripping the wire.

Raya found a stick at the base of the tree. Carefully, she wedged the stick between the hollow of the tree and the skeleton's hand. Once it was ready, she picked up the Gem fragment.

"Phew," she said, tossing the shard to Sisu. "Two down, three to go."

As Sisu caught the Gem piece, there was a small *poof!* The dragon vanished. In her place stood a woman with a thick mane of silvery, iridescent hair and Sisu's bright, curious eyes. She was dressed in loose-fitting clothes made from a blue-green fabric.

The woman looked down at herself in surprise. "I just shape-changed! Into people!"

"Dragons can do that?" Raya asked.

"This was my sister Pranee's thing!" Sisu began to march around, waving her arms and wobbling on her human legs. "Look at my people arms and my people face! Look at how close my butt is to my head. Now that you don't have to hide me, getting the rest of the gems is gonna be a breeze!"

Raya laughed. "Yeah, well, this one was easy, but the rest of them are being held by a bunch of no-good binturis."

"Binturi? That's not a very nice way to describe an old friend," said a cold voice near the entrance to the cavern.

Raya watched as Namaari and her soldiers entered the room.

CHAPTER SEVEN

Raya hadn't seen Namaari for six years, but she recognized her at once. Namaari's head was shaved on one side, just as it had been when she was a girl, and her face wore the same cold, haughty expression.

A surge of hatred washed through Raya at the sight of her old foe. "Namaari."

"What's dripping, dep la?" Namaari sneered. "Oh, I see you finally made a new friend. And here I was worried you were gonna end up becoming a cat lady. Like me."

At that, Namaari's Serlots, felines of unusual size from the Land of Fang, slinked into the chamber. She ran a hand over the head of her monstrous cat, who held perfectly still except for the tip of its tail, which flicked back and forth as if the Serlot was waiting for the chance to pounce.

"Something tells me you're not besties?" Sisu whispered to Raya.

"Stealing Dragon Gem pieces, are we? Why?" Namaari asked.

"What can I say? Bling is my thing," Raya retorted.

"I gotta admit, Raya, until a few months ago I thought you were stone. But then someone stole Fang's ancient manuscript—" Namaari started.

"Oh, is that why you're chasing me? And here I thought it was because you missed me," Raya interrupted, throwing Namaari the folded-up manuscript.

Namaari caught it. "Are you really looking for Sisu? What are you? Twelve?"

"I actually was looking for Sisu. Ooh, and guess what? I found her." Raya kept her voice steady. But her eyes darted around the room, searching for an escape.

Sisu glanced at Raya with alarm. Namaari looked startled.

"Say hi, Sisu," Raya said with a smile.

"Hi! It's very nice to meet you. And I love your hair— and your cats' . . . hair," Sisu said.

Namaari was not amused. "Take them," she commanded. Her warriors raised their crossbows.

With a deft kick, Raya tripped the wire connected to the skeleton's hand.

An ominous rumble came from overhead. The trapdoor

over the entrance fell open. A mountain of sand poured down on the Fang warriors and their Serlots.

As Namaari and her soldiers struggled to dig themselves out, Raya grabbed Sisu and swung them both back across the chasm. "Run!" she told Sisu.

Sisu fell onto all fours and tried to run on her hands and legs. She had forgotten she had a human body!

"Not like that! Two legs!" Raya hollered.

"Right!" Sisu hopped to her feet and hurried after Raya, weaving crazily on her unsteady legs.

Raya glanced back. Namaari and her gang were almost clear of the sand. She had to find another way to slow them down.

As they charged through the tunnel, Raya ran her hands along the walls, disturbing the toot-and-booms. The beetles swarmed, filling the tunnel with tiny, fiery explosions. Behind them, Raya heard curses and shouts as the Fang warriors dodged the blasts.

Moments later, Raya and Sisu burst out into the bright sunlight. Tuk Tuk was standing right where they'd left him. Raya had never been so happy to see her roly-poly friend.

She leapt onto his saddle, then pulled Sisu up behind her. "Tuk Tuk, go!" Raya screamed.

Tuk Tuk rolled into a ball, and they tore away.

As they barreled through narrow canyons, away from the

Tail ruins, Sisu looked back over her shoulder. "Who was that girl?" she asked.

"That's Namaari," Raya said through gritted teeth. "She's the backstabbing binturi that broke the world."

"Wow," Sisu said, looking back. "Those cats are really fast, huh?"

Raya looked back, too. Namaari and her soldiers were following. The Serlots bounded easily over the rocky landscape. They were closing the distance fast. Raya knew it would take more than just speed to escape them.

They had almost reached the Kumandran River. Ahead was the port of Tail, a sleepy cluster of wooden houses and ramshackle docks. A cluster of boats bobbed in the muddy water.

Raya suddenly had an idea. "What do cats and Druun have in common?" she said, thinking aloud.

Sisu paused, as if giving the question serious thought. "Um . . . they have no . . . souls!"

Raya raised an eyebrow. That wasn't exactly the answer she'd been expecting. "*And* they both hate water," she replied.

"Oh."

"Hold on!"

The Serlots were almost upon them. With a sudden swerve to the left, Raya steered Tuk Tuk over the edge of the embankment. They sailed down and landed with a splash in the water.

Tuk Tuk started swimming toward the nearest boat, a low wooden skiff with what appeared to be a giant crustacean on its roof.

Raya glanced back. Namaari and the Fang warriors had turned and were heading toward the docks.

When Raya reached the boat, she climbed aboard. Sisu and Tuk Tuk were close behind. "Hello?" Raya called. "Is anybody here?"

"Welcome to the world-famous Shrimporium!"

A boy popped up, startling her. He was dressed in a vest and loose-fitting pants. The hair above his forehead stood straight up in a cowlick.

"My name is Boun. I'll be your server today. Would you like to hear our daily specials?" he asked, producing chairs and a table like a magician performing a trick.

"Yes, please!" Sisu said, falling into a chair.

"We got shrimp. We got congee. We got a shrimp congee that won't quit," Boun recited.

"The captain! Where is the captain?" Raya cried.

"Let me get him," the boy replied.

He walked away a few paces, then turned back to them. "What's up, my new customers? I'm Captain

Boun, the owner, chef, and chief financial officer of the Shrimporium," the boy said. "How can I help you?"

With that, he started dancing. Sisu was very impressed. "Well, I'm Sisu and—"

"And we need to get to Talon. *Now,*" Raya insisted, watching Namaari and the Fang warriors arrive at the docks. In another minute, they would reach them.

Boun folded his arms. "I'm sorry, the Shrimporium is not a water taxi."

From her satchel, Raya produced blocks of jade. She held them out.

Boun's jaw fell open. "Toi! That's a lotta jade!"

Raya offered half to him. "Half now, half when we arrive in Talon. Deal?"

Boun grabbed the jade and shoved it into his pocket. "Clasp on to your congee. Today's special is . . ." He raised one eyebrow and smiled. *"To go."*

Tuk Tuk was about to take a bite of his food when Boun whisked it away!

Then the boy picked up a long pole and pushed the boat away from the dock. It inched out into the river with the approximate speed of oozing mud.

"Uh . . . Captain Boun? Does this thing go any faster?" Raya asked as the Serlots bounded onto the wooden docks.

"Whoa. You didn't tell me Fang was after you!" Boun shot back. "This is gonna cost extra!"

"Don't worry. I got it!" Sisu shouted. Without waiting for a reply, Sisu leapt over the side of the boat. They heard her splash.

Boun gaped. "What is she doing?"

Boun couldn't see Sisu from where he was standing. But Raya could. As soon as Sisu hit the water, she changed back into a dragon. She grabbed the bottom of the boat and pushed it down the river, using her tail as a propeller.

As the boat lurched forward, Boun and Raya looked at each other in amazement. "Whoa!"

"What is happening?" Boun cried.

"My friend's a really strong swimmer," Raya said, trying to sound as if this was the sort of thing that happened every day.

Namaari and her warriors arrived at the end of the dock just in time to see the boat speeding away. Namaari's face contorted in fury.

Raya grinned and gave her a big, friendly wave. "Bye-bye, binturi!"

Seething, Namaari watched them go.

"Princess Namaari," said a Fang officer, "they're after Gem pieces. Their next stop would be Talon."

Namaari considered this with narrowed eyes. Then she

dismissed the idea. "We're not following them to Talon. We're going back to Fang. I need to speak with Chief Virana."

Without waiting for a reply, Namaari turned her Serlot around and started for home.

CHAPTER EIGHT

The Shrimporium floated down the wide, muddy river. While Boun was busy in the kitchen, Raya peered into the murky water. Sisu had been down there for a long time. *Too long*, Raya thought.

"Sisu?" she whispered loudly, trying not to panic. "Sisu?"

At last, the dragon broke the surface, sighing in contentment. "Ah . . ."

"Please! Get out of there!" Raya begged.

Sisu shook water from her mane. She turned over and floated on her back, swishing her tail like a rudder. "I'm a water dragon," she informed Raya. "This is water. It's sorta my thing. You wanna to come in?"

"Someone could see you," Raya whispered, ignoring the invitation.

Sisu glanced over at Boun. He was banging on pots and pans as he cooked, dancing to the beat.

"Oh, do you mean Captain Pop-and-Lock over there? What? What, are you scared he's going to challenge me to a dance battle?" the dragon joked.

"Sisu, I saw people lose their minds over a Dragon Gem," Raya replied, dancing a bit so she wouldn't look odd talking over the side of the ship. "Can you imagine what they'd do over an actual dragon? Look, we need you to make this all work. Until we have all the gems, you have to stay human. Please."

"Wow. You've really got some trust issues."

"Look, my father blindly trusted people, and now he's stone," Raya replied.

With a sigh, Sisu climbed up onto the boat. As she did, she changed back into her human form. "Hey, we'll get your ba back. I got you, girl. Come on, who's your dragon? I mean, human. Because I'm gonna be human until—yeah, you get it."

Boun suddenly arrived, carrying four bowls and a steaming pot. He plunked the bowls down on the table and began ladling congee into them. "Okay, who's hungry?" he asked, pushing two bowls toward Raya and Sisu.

"Ooh! I am!" Sisu exclaimed, plopping down in a chair.

"Two house specials!" Boun spun a bottle of hot sauce

in his hand. "How spicy would you like it? Hot, hotter, or Boun-goes-the-dynamite?"

"Bring on the heat!" Sisu said.

The smell of the savory rice stew made Raya's mouth water. But she pulled Sisu's bowl away from her. "Yeah, no, no . . . I don't think so," she said.

"What are you doing?" asked Sisu.

Raya leaned close and whispered, "We don't know him. It could be poisoned."

Sisu frowned. "Why would he poison us?" she asked loudly.

"Yeah, why would I poison you?" asked Boun, clearly offended.

"First, to get my jade purse. Second, to steal my sword. And third . . . I don't know." Raya searched for a reason. "To kidnap my Tuk Tuk!"

"All good points," Boun conceded. "But if this is poison . . ." He lifted his bowl and slurped. "You're gonna die happy."

"Yeah. Thanks, but we've got our own eats." Raya took out some jerky and tore off a big, dry bite. It was like chewing boot leather, but she made a show of smiling as she swallowed it. She held out a piece of jerky to Sisu.

Sisu didn't notice. She had retrieved her bowl and was gulping down congee.

"This is delicious," she said, between bites. "By the way, not poison but . . ." Her face reddened. Her eyes started to stream as the peppers kicked in. "It's hot. . . . *IT'S REALLY HOT!* Water! Boun? Captain Boun? We need water on deck!" she yelled, fanning her mouth.

Raya shook her head and sighed. Sisu was far too trusting. She was going to have to teach the dragon to be on her guard if they were ever going to manage to save the world.

At that same moment, Namaari and her soldiers were nearing Fang. As they came over a rise, they saw dozens of stone dragons spread out before them. The statues were all that was left of the dragons that had fought the Druun five hundred years before.

The other soldiers rode on without stopping, but Namaari slowed her Serlot and paused. She looked with reverence at the great stone creatures. When no one was looking, she bowed to them. Then, urging her Serlot forward, she rode on.

Raya had hoped they might make it to the port of Talon by nightfall. But without Sisu pushing, the boat drifted only as fast as the current. She watched nervously as the sun sank lower and lower in the sky. By the time it dipped below the horizon, the land surrounding them was still, dense forest.

Druun were never far away, but they came out more at night. Raya, Sisu, and Boun watched from the deck of the boat as an eerie darkness swept through the trees near the shore.

Raya patted Tuk Tuk, who was trembling with fear. "I know, buddy."

"You know, during the day, you can almost forget they're here. But at night . . ." Boun shuddered, his eyes huge and frightened. "This why I never leave the boat."

"You're a smart kid," Raya said, remembering he was only a child.

"What are Druun, anyway?" Boun asked.

"A virus born from human discord. They've always been here, waiting for a moment of weakness to attack. They're, like, the opposite of dragons," Sisu said. "Instead of bringing water and life to the world, they're like a relentless fire that consumes everything in its wake until there's nothing left except ash and stone."

"They took my family," Boun said.

Sisu picked up some flowers and walked to the edge of the boat. "They took mine, too," she said as she dropped petals into the water.

Boun joined Sisu, who gave him some flowers. As he

began dropping petals, Raya came over. She dropped one single flower into the river, for her father. As the boat continued on, moving away from the Druun, the petals floated where they fell.

CHAPTER NINE

They arrived in the city of Talon at dusk. Despite the evening hour, the port was bustling. Over centuries, the Kumandran River had sunk lower and lower as the emerald water dwindled. Talon had adapted by building their docks lower and lower. Ladders connected the series of long, wooden walkways that extended into the river at odd angles.

A thriving marketplace had sprung up atop these many boardwalks. Stalls decorated with colorful lanterns were crammed side by side on the docks. As they floated into port, Raya saw merchants selling everything from vegetables and seafood to clothing and jewelry. The thick, humid air was heavy with the smells of food and the cries of vendors hawking their wares.

"Looks like we're here! So where are you guys headed

after Talon? I might be headed there, too," Boun said. "I mean, for a fee, of course."

"Of course," Raya said.

Sisu leaned over the edge of the boat, smiling approvingly. "Wow. What a smart way to Druun-proof your house. Build right on the water," she said. "People of Talon are geniuses."

Raya fastened on her sword. "Talon may look nice, but it's a hot spot for pickpockets and con artists," she warned.

Sisu turned her pockets inside out. "Lucky for me, empty pockets!"

"Okay, so here's the good news," Raya said. "I know where the Gem piece is. The bad news . . ." She remembered an imposing building, the largest in Talon, and a huge warrior with a long beard. "It's being held by the notorious chief of Talon, Dang Hai. What Dang Hai lacks in style, he makes up in mean."

"Gotcha," Sisu nodded. "Now we're just gonna have to turn up the charm. Let's go get him a gift!"

"Sisu, I think maybe it's safer for you to stay here on the boat," Raya said.

Sisu's mouth opened in surprise. "What?"

"Without you, we can't put the Gem back together," Raya explained.

"But I want to help," Sisu argued.

"I know, and you will, by staying safe," Raya said. "I'll be back before you know it."

Sisu looked frustrated, but Raya stood by what she had said. They couldn't take any chances on something happening to Sisu. Without the dragon, they had no hope of defeating the Druun. And Raya didn't want company on the mission. Get the Gem piece and get out—that was her plan. And for the plan to go smoothly, she trusted only herself.

Boun guided the boat to a dock and tied it off. "If you see any hungry faces, send 'em my way," he said.

"You got it, Captain," Raya promised as she and Tuk Tuk stepped off.

Compared to the empty, windswept landscape of Tail, Talon's night market was an assault on the senses. Bright colors, yammering voices, and pungent smells met Raya at every turn. As she and Tuk Tuk walked down the narrow alleys, they passed mouthwatering foods—colorful fruits, dumplings, skewers of meat, baskets full of fish, and platters piled high with rice cakes. Her stomach growled, but she pretended not to notice.

"All right, there's Dang Hai's house," Raya said, her eyes locked on a great wooden structure set high on stilts. A half dozen guards were stationed below it. "No detours until we score that Dragon Gem," Raya told Tuk Tuk.

Raya paused, scanning the joint. How was she going to get in?

A baby's cry interrupted her thoughts.

She turned. A plump toddler in grubby clothes sat on the ground nearby, wailing piteously.

"Whoa. What in the . . ." Raya looked around for its mother or father. There were no adults in sight. What was a baby doing out this late at night?

The baby held its little starfish hands out to Raya.

Raya sighed. No detours. That's what she'd said. On the other hand, she couldn't leave a sobbing toddler all alone in a dangerous city.

"Uh . . . okay . . ." Raya picked up the baby. It was surprisingly heavy. "Hey . . . baby, toddler, thing, whatever you're called," she said. "It's really late. What are you doing out here? Where are your parents?"

The baby smiled at Raya, showing two tiny teeth.

"Hey, whose baby—" Raya called out. At that moment, her eyes fell on Tuk Tuk. Three fuzzy, monkey-like creatures were perched on his saddle, rummaging in her satchel. Raya watched in horror as they removed the two Gem shards.

"What? Ongis?" she shouted. "Drop 'em!"

The Ongis leapt from Tuk Tuk's back, the Gem pieces clutched tightly in their little paws. In the same instant, the baby hissed, yanked Raya's hat down over her face, kicked

66

her in the chest, and then scuttled after the Ongis. The thieves disappeared into the marketplace.

"Really? A con *baby*!" Raya couldn't believe it. The baby was in on it!

With a growl, Raya chased after them, with Tuk Tuk on her heels. They raced down one alley after another, leaping from dock to dock. But each time Raya thought she'd almost caught them, the rascals escaped. Despite their innocent looks, the baby and the Ongis were clearly practiced criminals.

When the baby saw Raya was getting closer, she threw a diaper at her.

"Ah! Diaper!" Raya shouted.

At last, she and Tuk Tuk managed to corner the miniature menaces. The Ongis returned the Gem shards to Raya.

"Thanks," Raya said as she tucked the shards safely back into her satchel. "So it's none of my business. But using your baby charm to rip people off is super sketchy. All right, where's your family?"

The baby stuck out her tongue and blew a raspberry. Then she walked away with two of the Ongis. The littlest Ongi stayed, however, posing like a stone statue.

"Oh. Right," Raya said, realizing what had happened to the baby's family.

Raya watched the littlest Ongi join the rest. The group

shared some food. She looked up at Dang Hai's house, looming ahead.

"Hey," Raya said. "How would you like to earn some honest loot?"

Moments later, Raya watched from a hiding place as the baby toddled up to the guards at Dang Hai's house. When she caught their attention, the toddler fell onto her padded bottom, then stood up again, cooing adorably at the Ongis. As the guards watched the baby and the Ongis, Raya slipped past them into Dang Hai's palace. Inside, she found a stairway. She sneaked up the steps and emerged onto a wide balcony. A massive figure with a wide body and muscular arms stood there looking out at the view.

Raya pointed her sword at his back. "All right, Dang Hai," she said, making her voice low and threatening. "I'll take that Dragon Gem piece."

The man spun around, holding up his hands. But he wasn't the warrior Raya remembered. This man was much younger, with sleepy eyes and a slightly dopey face. "Whoa! I'm not Dang Hai! I'm Chai, the flower guy."

Raya kept her sword pointed at him. "Where's Dang Hai?" she demanded.

"He's right over there."

Chai pointed to a statue in the corner—a huge man with a long beard. The Druun had gotten Dang Hai, too.

"What? Who has his Gem piece?" Raya asked.

Chai shook his head. "The most vicious chief Talon has ever seen."

CHAPTER TEN

Back on the boat, Sisu paced impatiently. As Boun tidied up, she chewed over what Raya had said.

"This is giving me bad feels. Chief Dang Hai does not sound like someone you can smooth talk. Raya didn't even bring a gift." Sisu came to a decision. "That's it. I'm going shopping!"

She hopped down from the side of the boat, then stopped. "Oh, wait . . . I don't have any money."

"You're an adult," Boun said. "You could just put it on credit."

Sisu looked at him with interest. "Oooh. What's credit?"

"It's kinda like a promise," Boun explained. "You take what you want now, and you promise you'll pay it back later."

Sisu's face lit up. "Pay it back later . . . what an amazing concept! Thanks, Captain Boun!"

She started into the market, enjoying all the sights and smells. There were so many nice things to choose from!

Sisu grabbed some skewers of meat off a grill. At the next stall, she spotted a beautiful silk robe and draped it over her arm. "I'll be buying this with credit. Ooh, Dang Hai's gonna love this. Credit, please," she called to the stunned merchant. "Oh, I like that. Uh, yeah. I'll be using credit. Yes. I love credit!"

Sisu continued through the marketplace, loading her arms with sweet treats, jade necklaces, and rolls of silk. Then she set off to find Raya so they could deliver the gifts to Dang Hai.

She hadn't gone far when she heard an angry shout. "Hey! You!"

Sisu stopped. A group of merchants were following her. They formed a circle around her, blocking her path.

"Are you going to pay for any of that?" one demanded, pointing to the pile of goods in Sisu's arms.

"Oh, right, right. No, this is on credit," Sisu explained. "Yeah, I'm gonna pay you back later."

"Pay us back later?" another exclaimed. "We don't know you!"

"You have no credit here. Pay us now!" a third merchant demanded.

Sisu looked around at their furious faces. "Now? I don't have anything," she admitted. "But if I could find my girl Raya, she has a sword. Dried eats. Two Dragon Gem pieces—" Sisu broke off, realizing she'd said too much. "No, we don't. What? Who said that?" she added quickly.

"You better pay up, binturi!" the first merchant continued, and the others chimed in.

"This isn't a charity!"

"Who do you think you're stealing from?"

Sisu backed away, feeling frightened and confused. Things hadn't been like this back when the lands were united as Kumandra. What was she supposed to do?

As the angry merchants closed in, a tiny old woman in a tall purple hat suddenly appeared at Sisu's side.

"Nee! Nee! Get away from her!" the old woman cried, slapping at the merchants' hands. "Can't you see she's new in town?"

At once, the merchants stepped back, looking chastened. Sisu turned to the woman with a grateful smile.

"Come, dear. Don't be afraid. It's okay," the old woman said, leading her away from the market.

"Those folks were, like, crazy mad," Sisu said as they

walked through Talon. "I just wanted to bring some gifts to the Talon chief, Dang Hai."

The woman raised her eyebrows in mild interest. "Is that who you're looking for, dear? I know exactly where he is."

"You do?" Sisu said.

"Mmm-hmm. I'll take you there." The woman motioned forward.

"See!" Sisu exclaimed. "That's what I've been trying to tell my girl Raya. But she's all like, 'You can't trust people. Don't talk to anyone. I only eat terrible foods I dried myself.'"

As they walked, two huge men appeared out of nowhere and flanked the old woman and Sisu like bodyguards, following alongside. Sisu turned and gave each of them a big smile. But the men just stared ahead coldly.

They came to a great stone gateway. The two men cranked a wheel to lower a drawbridge. The old woman steered Sisu onto the bridge. "Come, dear. Chief Dang Hai is just outside the city, beyond the gates," she explained.

"Away from the water, huh?" Sisu said, surprised. "Wow. He really likes living on the edge."

They opened the huge set of doors to the final gate. Beyond the city was the dense, dark jungle. Compared to the bustle of Talon, the deep buzz of insects seemed ominous.

With relief, Sisu spotted another figure standing close by in the darkness.

"Hi there, Dang Hai," Sisu said, starting toward him. "I'm Sisu. I've come here to offer you some—"

Sisu broke off. The person was made of stone!

Sisu glanced around. As her eyes adjusted to the darkness, she realized she was surrounded by stone statues. This wasn't Dang Hai's home. It wasn't a home at all. It was a graveyard.

An ominous, hissing rattle sounded somewhere nearby. Sisu's blood ran cold. A Druun emerged from the trees, coming right toward her. But just as it was about to engulf her, a flash of blue light pushed it back. Sisu turned to see the old woman and the bodyguards back by the gate. The woman was holding up a Dragon Gem shard. Its glow was repelling the Druun. Sisu had been tricked! The woman was Dang Hu, Dang Hai's mother—and the merciless chief of Talon.

Dang Hu narrowed her eyes. "Now you're going to tell me where I can find those other Dragon Gem pieces. Or"—she nodded toward the Druun—"I'll have to leave you outside with that . . . thing. Take your pick."

"But I trusted you," Sisu said, stunned.

"Big mistake," Dang Hu replied, stepping backward. Her bodyguards began to close the gate. "Better talk fast. It looks hungry."

Sisu watched as more Druun emerged from the trees. "No, no, no," she said.

But Dang Hu lowered her Gem shard, and the Druun rushed in. Then—

WHAM!

The gate suddenly blasted open. Raya rolled through on a speeding Tuk Tuk and swooped Sisu up into the saddle.

"Raya!" Sisu cried with relief.

"Stop her!" Dang Hu roared.

"Sisu, I told you to stay on the boat!" Raya exclaimed.

"Sorry!" Sisu shouted.

As they passed Dang Hu, Raya leaned down and swiped the Dragon Gem fragment from her hand.

"Hold on to this for me, will you?" Raya said, handing the shard to Sisu.

Raya barreled toward the gate while the bodyguards tried again to close the doors. But as the Gem shard touched Sisu's hands, a blast of fog covered everything, scaring away the Druun. In the confusion, Raya and Sisu dodged Dang Hu and her bodyguards, making their escape back through the city. It wasn't long before they were rolling onto the docks.

"Fog?" Raya exclaimed.

"Yeah, that was my brother Jagan's magic," Sisu said.

"Okay, three down, two to go!" Raya said as they hopped

on board the Shrimporium. "All right, Captain Boun. Next stop, Spine—"

Raya broke off as a bowl whizzed past her head. She had ducked just in time. Boun, the Ongis, and the con baby were gathered around the table. The three animals and the baby were gulping down congee like it was water.

"Thanks for the new customers!" Boun exclaimed.

Raya smiled. "Yeah, I sort of promised to buy them all the congee they could eat."

"Well, we're stuck with them for a while. Because Ongis have nine stomachs," Boun said.

"Oh, toi," Raya said as she and Sisu joined them at the table.

"I can't believe it," Sisu said. "That old lady was really going to hurt me."

"Well, I'm sorry, Sisu, that's what the world is now. You can't trust anyone."

The baby looked at them and smiled.

"Does that include babies?" Sisu asked.

"Uh, well . . . ," Raya began.

"She's so cute. I mean look at those cheeks!" Sisu said as the baby reached up and lovingly grabbed her face. "Hi, I'm Sisu."

"Soo-soo," repeated the baby, who was now leaping onto Sisu's face.

"Aw, she loves my face," Sisu said.

"Watch out she doesn't steal your teeth. Here, let me help you." Raya gently pulled the toddler away.

"Oh, that's so sweet. . . . Okay, too much sweetness, too much sweetness! It's too much!" Sisu told the baby.

But as the boat moved out into the current, Sisu looked back as the lights of Talon receded into the distance. She couldn't shake the image of Dang Hu and her henchmen closing the gate to leave her with the Druun. This wasn't the world Sisu knew. Her dragon mind struggled to comprehend it. Hopefully, things would be different in the Land of Spine.

CHAPTER ELEVEN

After leaving Tail, Namaari and her soldiers raced back to Fang, riding their Serlots through the night to reach their homeland. Namaari's rage at losing Raya burned steadily, driving her on. But even in her fury, Namaari's mind was calculating.

Raya was stealing Gem shards from enemy lands. That could only mean she would eventually come to Fang. And that had given Namaari an idea. But first, she had to consult with her mother, Chief Virana.

Arriving back at the palace on the island of Fang, Namaari found her mother in the throne room, talking with her generals. Virana and her advisors were leaning over a map of Kumandra, studying it together. Namaari paused in the doorway to listen.

"Chief Virana, we're running out of room," the general said. "We need to expand to the mainland."

"And how do you suppose we handle the Druun, General Atitāya?" Virana replied. "Without proper protection, it would be a death sentence for our people."

"I might have a solution for that, Mother," Namaari said.

Virana looked up. When she saw daughter standing in the doorway, her face brightened. "My little morning mist," Virana said, holding her hands out to welcome her. "It's good to see you home."

"I located Raya," Namaari told her. "She's out stealing Gem pieces."

"What?" Virana looked startled. She glanced at her own Dragon Gem shard, which was firmly fixed in the end of her long golden staff.

"I'd like to take the royal army and intercept her in Spine," Namaari said.

Virana arched an eyebrow. "Well, if she's going into Spine, I doubt there will be much left of her to intercept."

"She's more capable than you realize," Namaari replied. "We have to stop her."

Virana studied her daughter's angry face. "Walk with me," she said.

With a swish of her silk cape, Virana turned from the

throne room. Namaari followed her mother outside. Side by side, they walked along the promenade. The generals followed behind them at a respectful distance.

Fang's elegant stone palace sat on a terrace at the center of the island. Below it sat the orderly village and farmland, the lush green fields fed by water from the Kumandran River. Although the territory of Fang was vast, the entire population lived on the small island. A wide canal separated them from the mainland—and, more importantly, protected them from the Druun.

"Look around," Virana said, gesturing to the land around them. "We made all this by making smart decisions, not emotional ones. We are safe. Our canal protects us from those monsters. I don't think it's wise to risk yourself when you don't have to."

"But you heard the general," Namaari argued. "We're running out of space. We need to expand. If we had all the Gem pieces, we could do that safely. You're right. This isn't an emotional decision—it's the only decision we can make to secure Fang's future."

Chief Virana paused, thinking. "Namaari, you've truly grown into the leader I raised you to be." She summoned her general with a wave. "General Atitāya, ready the royal army for my daughter's command."

"Thank you, Mother," Namaari said, bowing. "I won't let you down."

Namaari smiled, thinking of how surprised Raya would be when she showed up in Spine.

CHAPTER TWELVE

Far down the river, the Shrimporium floated onward. As Raya and the others left behind the dense jungle and river markets of Talon, the land rose steeply into tall, slender mountains. The air turned cold. They passed through silent forests of giant bamboo. When Raya started to see snow on the ground, she knew they were nearing Spine.

Spine was best known for its brutish warriors—giants wielding battle-axes, who could fell a tree in one blow. To get past them, Raya knew she would have to be at the top of her game. As she cleaned her sword with a slice of lime, checking the blade's sharpness, she tried to clear her mind.

It wasn't easy. Ever since the baby and the Ongis had come aboard, the Shrimporium had been in a state of pandemonium. The rascals shoved congee and condiments into their mouths at every opportunity.

"Hey! Stop eating!" Boun yelled, chasing them off for the umpteenth time.

As they scampered away, the Ongis knocked hot sauce onto Tuk Tuk's food. He took a big bite, then knocked Raya over trying to get to the side of the ship for water.

"Sorry, buddy. I got this," Raya said, deciding to take matters into her own hands.

"Did you just throw a shrimp at me?" Boun yelled at one of the Ongis. "That's not even edible!" he exclaimed at another. "Don't look at me like that, you fuzzy garbage can!"

Raya walked over with a big smile. "Hey, guys. Do you want to play hide-and-seek?" she asked.

Tuk Tuk, the baby, and the Ongis nodded.

Raya covered her eyes. "All right, ready? One . . . two . . ."

The baby and the Ongis scurried away to hide. Even Tuk Tuk tried to hide, though he wasn't very good at it.

"Thanks," Boun whispered.

"Two and a half . . . three . . ." Raya counted slowly. She sat down next to Sisu and whispered, "Remind me to never have kids."

"Being people is hard," Sisu said.

"Yep," Raya agreed. Leaning back, she called, "Six . . . seven . . ."

"You have small heads, no tails. You lie to get what you want," Sisu went on. "Like the Talon chief back there."

"Yeah, well, the world's broken. You can't trust anyone," Raya said.

"Or maybe the world's broken *because* you don't trust anyone," Sisu retorted.

"You sound just like my ba," Raya said.

"Well, he sounds like a smart man," said Sisu.

"Yeah. He was. I really wanted to believe him. I really wanted to believe we could be Kumandra again."

"And we can," Sisu said.

Raya leaned forward. "Literally thousands of people turned to stone would argue otherwise."

Sisu wouldn't let it go. "That doesn't mean you shouldn't try."

Raya's composure crumbled. Why couldn't she make Sisu understand? "And I did. And you know what happened? I got kicked in the back by someone who gave me a 'gift.' Look around. We're a world of orphans because people couldn't stop fighting over a gem. Want to know why the other dragons didn't come back? It's because people don't deserve them."

"But you can change that," Sisu said.

"No, Sisu. I am done trying. Kumandra is a fairy tale.

The only thing important to me now is bringing my ba back."

The ship came to a stop. "Um," Boun interrupted. "I think we're in Spine."

Raya glanced up. Through the parting clouds, she could see an imposing village sitting above them on the hillside. A tall fence of sharpened bamboo surrounded it, but she could make out the houses. Decorated with the horns and tusks of massive beasts, they reminded her of giant beetles.

The dock was long gone. All that was left was a row of broken piles. As Boun steered the boat toward the shore, Sisu suddenly leapt overboard, carrying a large pot full of Boun's congee.

She hopped across the piles, then stormed up the hillside, headed for the village.

"Sisu!" Raya yelled.

"Hey! My congee!" Boun said in alarm.

"Don't go anywhere. I'll be right back." Grabbing her sword and the satchel of Gem shards, Raya chased after Sisu.

"Sisu! Come back! Please. What are you doing?" she called.

Sisu didn't even look around. "I'm going to show you that you're wrong!"

"How? By getting squashed by a bunch of Spine rage heads?" Raya asked in disbelief.

"No." Sisu marched right up to the tall wooden doors. "By proving to you that if you want to get someone's trust, you have to give a little trust first." She grasped the huge round knocker on the gate and started knocking.

"Sisu, don't!" Raya cried.

WHOOSH! A huge burlap sack sprang up from beneath their feet, trapping them both inside.

Squashed together in the bag, Raya glared at Sisu.

"In hindsight, maybe I was a little hasty," Sisu said at last. She held up the soup pot. "But . . . who's hungry? No? I'll leave you alone."

By evening, they found themselves in a low, smoky hut. Raya and Sisu had been trussed, tied back-to-back, and hung like sausages. They dangled at the end of a long rope that had been tied to a giant tusk.

"Okay . . . where are we?" Raya looked around for their attacker. A small fire burned in the fireplace, casting shadows across the walls. But aside from Raya and Sisu, the cabin was empty.

Raya wiggled her fingers to see if she could slip them out of her bonds. But the ropes had been tied too tightly. If only she could find some way to cut through them . . .

Raya spied her sword leaning against the wall, just out of reach.

"Interesting choice of digs," Sisu noted.

At that moment, the door burst open. An enormous man strode into the room. His boulder-like shoulders were so large they made his head seem tiny. He was dressed from head to toe in heavy furs. His long black hair was limp with grease, and he wore a patch over one eye. What caught Raya's attention most, though, was the ax in his hands—huge, curved, and deadly looking.

With a roar, the giant slammed his ax into the wall. "You two must be dung of brain to think you could steal Spine's Dragon Gem."

Raya flinched. But she tried to play it cool. "Gem? Who said anything about gems? We have no interest in gems," she told him.

In reply, the warrior picked up Raya's satchel and turned it over. The Gem shards from Heart, Tail, and Talon spilled onto a table.

"Okay, yeah. I can see how that makes me look like a liar," Raya said. Despite the chill air, she was sweating.

"Actually, I think it was the lying that made you look like a liar," Sisu pointed out.

The man glared at Raya and Sisu with his one good eye.

Then he laughed. It was not a friendly laugh. The sound sent chills down Raya's spine.

Sisu giggled nervously. "I'm not sure what's funny," she admitted.

"Your fear is like a delectable nectar feeding the tum-tum of my soul," the man replied. He had a strangely formal way of speaking that was at odds with his brutish appearance. "It's good. It tastes like . . . mango."

Sisu brightened. "Ooh, I love mango."

The man put his face right up to Sisu's. "OF COURSE YOU LOVE MANGO," he spat. "Only a tongueless cretin wouldn't."

"Oh, toi." Sisu stopped giggling and shrank away.

"It's been such a long time since I've last peered into the eyes of a trembling enemy." His gaze was distant. "Where has the time gone? It's been so long. . . ."

"He seems lonely," Sisu whispered to Raya.

"NO! I'm not lonely. I'm a Spine warrior," the man roared, pounding his chest. "I was born and bred to do only one thing—to invoke fear and crush the skulls of my enemies."

"That's actually two things," Sisu pointed out.

"RAWR!" the man roared.

"Ah!" Sisu shrieked.

"Ha ha." The brute chuckled. "Look at your face."

"Hey. What do you plan on doing with us?" Raya asked, still looking for some way to escape.

"Oh, it's going to be bad. Horrifying," the man replied. "It'll take me two weeks to clean up."

"You have no idea, do you?" Raya said, calling his bluff.

"Yes, I do!" he exclaimed. "I'm formulating this gruesome plan in my head. It makes me sick just thinking about it. You just wait. Until then, why don't you just *hang around*?" he joked. "Good one, huh? Ha ha."

CRASH! Tuk Tuk smashed through the door in an explosion of splintering wood. Boun, the baby, and the Ongis were on his back. With savage yells, they leapt onto the stunned barbarian and clung and clawed like a pack of wild animals. Within seconds, the Ongis had him tied up.

The man hardly seemed to know what had hit him. He looked around, dazed, at his tiny attackers. "A little one?" he said when he spotted the con baby.

"All right!" Sisu cheered.

"Good work, Captain Boun," Raya said as Boun used her sword to cut her and Sisu free.

But Boun looked worried. "Fang's here," he murmured to Raya.

The baby and the Ongis hissed at the mention of Fang.

Raya hadn't expected them so soon. "What?"

From outside the village walls, Namaari's voice rang out

through the frozen air. "People of Spine. We are hunting for Raya, a fugitive from Heart. Send her out, or we're coming in!"

Raya glanced out the cabin window. She expected to see warriors emerging from the other houses, ready for battle. But the village was still and silent.

She turned to him in surprise. "You're the only one here?"

"My people battled the Druun with valor . . . but lost," he admitted.

Raya looked around the Spine warrior's cabin and spotted an empty crib. Glancing at Sisu, she put the Gem pieces back in her satchel and handed it to her. She couldn't risk losing them. There was only one thing to do.

"Okay, the Fang gang's here for me, not for you," she told Sisu and the others. "If I can distract them, you guys can get out of here."

Sisu looked worried. "You're going to fight an entire army?"

"No, I'm just going to stall them," Raya said. "I know how to push Namaari's buttons. Once you guys are clear, I'm out of there."

She turned and knelt down before the Spine warrior, looking him right in the eye. "What's your name?"

"The moniker given to me is Tong," he replied.

"Okay, Tong, you don't know me, I don't know you,"

Raya said. "But I'm sure that you know a back door or a way out of here, and it's really important that my friends stay safe. Okay? So I am sincerely asking you, will you help us? Please."

Tong gazed at her for a long moment, as if he was trying to look into her soul. Then he gave a single silent nod.

Raya sliced through his ropes with her sword. She prayed she was doing the right thing.

As Tong prepared to lead her friends through the village, toward a secret exit, Raya walked alone to the village gate.

"Okay. Note to self: don't die." Raya took a deep breath and put on her hat.

As she neared the gate, she could hear Namaari shout, "Burn them out!"

Behind her stood dozens of soldiers holding crossbows loaded with flaming arrows. They were one moment away from burning down the village.

But as Raya opened the gate, the soldiers lowered their arrows.

"Hey there, Princess Undercut," Raya said. "Fancy meeting you here."

Namaari bared her teeth. "You and those Dragon Gem pieces are coming with me."

Raya's hand went to her hilt. "Hmm. My sword here says we're not."

At once, the Fang soldiers again raised their weapons. Raya smirked. "Yeah, I knew you couldn't handle rolling solo," she needled Namaari. "You're nothing without your band."

The soldiers started forward. Raya held her breath. Would her bluff work?

Namaari held up a hand, commanding her troops to stop. "Stand down. This shouldn't take long." She turned to Raya and raised her weapon, a spear topped with a deadly-looking foot-long knife.

Raya smiled. She removed her cape and drew her sword, too, and charged. But Namaari was ready. Their swords clashed with a bitter clang. Raya's feet slid over the snow as she fought to gain the advantage.

At last, Raya threw Namaari off. With a lash of her whiplike sword, she yanked the spear from Namaari's hands. "Did you need that, dep la?" she said.

Namaari landed a kick that sent Raya to the ground. She caught her sword easily, then threw it away. "Nah."

"Looks like somebody's been taking classes," Raya teased, then she charged Namaari again. Namaari was ready with fresh blows and kicks. Raya fended her off. But Namaari pressed harder.

At last, Raya saw a split-second opening. She spun around, aiming a kick at Namaari's head. But Namaari caught her

Young Raya has trained her whole life to become a
Guardian of the Dragon Gem, and she's about to prove
she's ready.

The Dragon Gem lies safely inside the Heart Fortress
at the top of a rock formation in the Land of Heart,
Raya's home.

Raya relies on her best friend, Tuk Tuk, for help—though he is easily distracted by yummy bugs.

Raya's father, Chief Benja, tests her skills in the Chamber of the Dragon Gem. Raya passes! She becomes a Guardian of the Dragon Gem, like her father.

The Dragon Gem holds the last remnants of dragon magic. But one tragic day, the Dragon Gem is broken!

The other lands of Kumandra—Fang, Talon, Spine, and Tail—each steal a piece. Chief Benja and many others are turned to stone!

Since that day, Raya has looked far and wide for the last dragon, Sisu, who is the only one who can help her save the world.

Once she finds Sisu, Raya will search all of Kumandra to find the stolen Dragon Gem pieces.

Sisu has been sleeping at the end of a river—the last one Raya visits—and she wakes up hungry!

Finding Sisu gives Raya hope. She's ready to do whatever it takes to get the Gem pieces back...

...and she is a skilled fighter!

But Raya can't do it alone.
She meets Boun in Tail,
Baby Noi and the Ongis in
Talon, and Tong in Spine.

Raya also faces her enemy, Namaari, whose betrayal of Raya led to the breaking of the Dragon Gem.

Namaari only cares about protecting her mother, Chief Virana, and their home, the Land of Fang.

Raya is focused on saving the world and bringing back her father, and Sisu and the Gem pieces are her last hope.

Namaari doesn't want Raya to get the Gem pieces, but Raya is ready to fight for them if she has to.

foot, throwing her off balance. She kicked Raya in the ribs. Hard.

Raya doubled over. Pain shot through her.

"Why are you stealing Gem pieces?" Namaari demanded.

Forcing herself erect, Raya spied Tong and the rest of the group escaping from the cabin. "Oh, I'm trying to get a matching set," she joked.

With a snarl, Namaari came at Raya again. This time her foot caught Raya in the chin. Raya landed on her back. Stars swirled before her eyes. She gasped, trying to catch her breath.

But she wouldn't give Namaari the satisfaction of giving in. "You didn't happen to bring Fang's gem, did you?" she asked through gritted teeth. Again, she struggled to her feet.

And again, Namaari knocked her down.

Raya struggled to rise, but she couldn't. Still, she egged Namaari on. "No? Never mind, I'll just swing by and grab it later."

"Oh, I'm going to enjoy this." Namaari picked her up. Raya braced herself for the final blow.

It never came. A blast of thick fog suddenly rolled over them like a blanket.

The dragon bounded through the open gate. Her head swung side to side as she spewed fog through her open jaws.

With cries of fear, the Fang soldiers threw down their

weapons and ran. Sisu advanced until she was standing right over Namaari. She glared, baring her needlelike teeth.

Raya heard a small noise. Glancing over, she saw Tong, Boun, the baby, and the Ongis standing among the trees. They gaped at Sisu in open-mouthed shock.

Raya dragged herself to her feet. Wrapping her arms tightly over her bruised ribs, she limped over to them.

"Yep, she's a dragon," she said. "Let's go. Go! Come on!"

Tong put an arm under her shoulders and helped her away.

Namaari seemed frozen to the spot. When her gaze met Sisu's, her eyes filled with tears.

With everyone at a safe distance, Sisu turned and bounded away, leaving Namaari staring after her in wonder.

CHAPTER THIRTEEN

With relief, the fugitives climbed onto the Shrimporium. Boun pushed off from the bank. The boat moved slowly into the current, weighed down by its heavy load of passengers. Sisu jumped into the water, grabbed the bottom of the boat and fanned her tail. The Shrimporium sped off down the river.

Raya looked back at Spine to make sure they weren't being followed. As she turned forward again, something small and slimy hit her forehead. "Did someone just hit me with a shrimp tail?" she asked in disbelief.

Boun, with the con baby at his side, stared at her. His arms were folded tightly across his chest. "So when were you going to tell us she was Sisu?"

"Technically, you always knew she was Sisu," Raya pointed out.

This answer didn't sit well. Another shrimp tail hit Raya. "Seriously?" she said.

Sisu climbed back on board, not bothering to change into her human form.

Tong stepped forward. "Why are you here, divine water dragon?" he asked Sisu.

Sisu smiled. "Isn't that obvious, big guy? My girl Raya and I are gonna fix the world. Bring everyone back."

"You're going to bring everyone back?" Boun asked. "I want to help."

"I'm sorry, I can't let you do that." Raya said. "It's too dangerous."

"You're not the only one who lost family to the Druun," he replied quietly, kneeling before Sisu. "Please let me help you."

Raya's heart went out to the boy. She'd been only a year or two older than Boun when she'd lost her own ba. She'd never forgotten how alone and frightened she felt.

A second later, the con baby and the Ongis knelt and bowed, too.

"I, too, wish to join this fellowship of Druun butt-kickery," Tong declared, lowering onto his knees. He removed something from a pouch at his waist and held it out.

Raya's heart skipped a beat. It was the Spine Dragon

Gem shard. Sisu gently took it from Tong, and her eyes brightened.

A drop of rain splashed down. Then another. Then more.

As the sprinkle turned into a downpour, Sisu lifted her face to the sky. "My big brother Pengu's magic . . ."

All of a sudden, Sisu bounded into the air. Raya and the others watched as the dragon ran across the sky. She raced in circles and loop-the-loops as gracefully as a fish swimming through water. She climbed higher and higher, her feet scrambling over the raindrops as if she was running up stairs. As the clouds parted, the sun beamed down on her with golden light.

Raya felt as if a weight had been lifted off her. She was flooded with feelings she hadn't known in years—joy, wonder, and, most of all, hope.

When Sisu had finished her skylarking, she dove straight down, plunging into the river. *SPLASH!* Raya and the others took cover behind Tong, who was soaked.

Sisu surfaced and looked right at Raya and grinned. Raya grinned back.

So that's what it was like when the dragons walked among us, she thought. *What an amazing world it must have been.*

"All right, Captain Boun. To Fang!" Raya commanded with a smile.

"You got it!" Boun replied. And they were off!

CHAPTER FOURTEEN

With Spine's Gem fragment now in hand, they were only one shard away from completing the Dragon Gem. But this one would be the hardest to get.

Raya rolled a map out on the table. "All right, everyone. Here's the plan. The last Gem piece is in Fang," Raya said, pointing to the island, a tiny speck in the great Kumandran River, right were the dragon's fang would be. "The most heavily guarded of the five lands. Now they're protected by an artificial canal that separates them from the rest of the world. The only way in or out is by water. Lucky for us, we have a magic water dragon."

As the others listened, Raya continued to outline her plan. The people of Fang favored white garments. Raya and her team would arrive at night, emerging from the water disguised as citizens. She felt certain they would pass through the village undetected.

"Now the palace will be swarming with Fang soldiers," she explained, knowing Namaari would be expecting them. "To sneak past them, we'll need to—"

"I got this, guys. I'll take out the first wave," Boun interrupted. As Boun explained his plan, he bounced around, demonstrating some dubious martial arts moves. "Tong will follow up with his giant ax of bad-axery."

In Boun's vision, Tong swung a battle-ax at a group of imaginary soldiers.

"And then come the Ongis and that crazy con baby"— according to Boun, they would sneak into the palace and steal the Gem shard from Chief Virana when she wasn't looking—"who will toss the Gem to the mighty Sisudatu . . . rawr . . . and then . . . bye-bye, binturis." Boun looked to Raya for approval. "Super flow plan, am I right?"

Raya frowned. "Uh, no. Yeah, that's not flow. That's a clog."

"I agree," Sisu said. "Here's my plan. . . ."

As the others listened, Sisu laid out her plan. "We'll infiltrate Fang, confront Namaari . . . and offer her something nice and go, 'Hey. Want to help us save the world? Because all it takes is one Gem piece!'"

At that point, Sisu continued, Namaari would say, "Yes! I've been waiting for someone to ask me! Here ya go!" After handing over the Gem piece, she'd skip off with Sisu. "Best friends forever!"

Sisu beamed around at the group.

They gazed back at her in dismay. Raya had always known the dragon was a bit too trusting. But this plan was total lunacy.

"Great idea, but, um . . . I think I'd rather go with Boun's plan," she said.

"What?" Sisu seemed surprised.

"Yes!" Boun shouted.

"Why?" Sisu asked.

"Because it's Fang," Raya said.

"Their blades are specially designed for the stabbing of backs," Tong agreed.

"If it weren't for them, none of this would have happened," Boun chimed in. "They're the worst."

Even the con baby had an opinion, which she communicated with a sound of disgust.

Sisu gazed at them with disappointment. "If we're just honest with her, down deep, I got a feeling she wants to fix the world as badly as we do."

"You weren't there when Namaari betrayed me," Raya shot back. She remembered the feeling of Namaari's boot in her back that day in the Chamber of the Dragon Gem. "We're sticking with my plan."

Sisu frowned. Although the sun was shining brightly, the sky suddenly opened. Sheets of rain splashed down. In seconds, everyone was soaked.

"Whoa. Uh, what's with the downpour?" Raya asked Sisu.

"Come on. I need to show you something." Without warning, Sisu grabbed Raya and began climbing the raindrops into the sky.

"So . . . what do we do now?" Boun asked.

Tong shrugged.

From above, Raya glanced down at the boat. She saw the small round faces of Tong, Boun, the baby, Tuk Tuk, and the Ongis tilted up toward them, watching curiously.

In seconds, they had left the boat behind. The dragon raced through the air, her body rippling like a wave. On her back, Raya clung to Sisu's fur for dear life.

On they flew. The sun lit the rain clouds from behind, making them glow with inner magic. Below, Raya saw the Kumandran River snaking through the hills and forests. Sisu seemed to be following it.

Raya was in awe. "Where are you taking me?"

Sisu didn't reply. Just then, the clouds ahead parted. Raya saw an island in the middle of the river with a familiar shape rising up from it—a great natural stone archway. With a pang, she realized Sisu was taking her to Heart. She was taking Raya home.

When they reached the Chamber of the Dragon Gem, Sisu sailed through the open roof. She landed lightly inside, and Raya climbed down from her back.

A lump rose in Raya's throat as she looked around. The once-glorious home of the Dragon Gem lay in ruins. Stone pillars were scattered across the floor like fallen trees. Here was the crack where the Druun had emerged, now grown over with vines. Shafts of sunlight came through holes in the crumbling walls, puncturing the gloom.

She didn't want to see it this way, a reminder of how badly they had failed. "Sisu, why did you bring me here?" she asked, fighting back tears.

"This is where it all happened," Sisu replied softly.

Raya swiped at her eyes. "Yeah, I know. I was there."

"No, this is where it all happened five hundred years ago." Sisu pulled down some foliage that was covering four great dragon statues. Her eyes were full of love and sadness. "I want you to meet my brothers and sisters," she told Raya. "The *real* mighty ones. I miss them."

Raya looked at the stone dragons. For the first time, she realized they looked like Sisu, though they were much bigger. "I never knew they were here," she said, bowing.

"See that classy looking one over there?" Sisu said, pointing to the dragon across from her. "That's Amba. I get my glow from her."

She turned to another statue. "And that's Pranee. She's the shape-shifter. Jagan—fog." Sisu looked up at the dragon above her. "And Pengu. He's our big brother. He brings the rain." Sisu sighed. "We were the last dragons."

Raya moved closer as Sisu began her story.

"All the other dragons had been turned to stone," Sisu told her. "We were drowning in a sea of Druun."

In her mind's eye, Raya could see it—five dragon siblings gathered together on this very spot. She pictured them forming a tight circle as the storm of hissing, howling Druun raged.

"And my oldest brother, Pengu, refused to accept defeat. This is where we'd make our last stand, united," said Sisu. "So, one by one, they combined all their magic, creating the Dragon Gem."

First, Pengudatu conjured up a sphere of water that contained all the power of rain. Amba placed her hand on it, adding her glow. Jagan breathed his fog into it. Pranee gave it shape-shifting power. When they were finished, the sphere of water solidified into the Dragon Gem. The four dragons, with the Gem in their hands, turned to Sisu.

"I don't know why they chose me. It could have been any

of us," Sisu explained. "All I know is I trusted them and they trusted me. And so . . ."

They placed the Gem into her hands. As they let go, they turned to stone.

"When they put their faith in me, it empowered me beyond anything I could imagine. The same can happen with Namaari."

Raya looked down. "I really wish I could believe that. I once thought we could be friends."

"After all this, maybe you can be."

"Even if she wanted to help us, how could I possibly trust her?"

"But if somehow you could, you wouldn't just bring your ba back," Sisu said. "You'd also bring back his dream: Kumandra."

Raya was silent. She wanted to believe Sisu, she really did. But she could never forgive Namaari for what she'd done.

Raya felt Sisu's eyes on her as she waited for an answer. Raya turned away, pretending to study a flower growing up from a crack in the floor. As she reached down and plucked it, Raya suddenly longed to see her ba. For six years, she had avoided Heart. But now she wanted nothing more than to see his face again.

Chief Benja was still in the same place, halfway across the

Heart Bridge. Like all statues left behind by the Druun, he stood with his eyes closed, his head bowed. A little pool of rainwater had collected in his cupped hands. Sisu watched silently as Raya floated a flower in that rainwater.

She touched his stone fingers. They were so cold, so unlike the strong, warm hand that had once held her own. But his face was so familiar, every curve and line. She willed him to open his eyes and look at her, to wrap her in his arms again.

"Do you think he would even recognize me? So much has changed," she said to Sisu.

Sisu nodded. "Of course he will."

"You remind me of him."

"Oh yeah? Strong, good-looking, with impeccable hair."

Raya laughed. "Hopeful," she said, then she turned back to her father and gently held his hands.

At that moment, Raya felt she would do anything—anything at all—to have her ba back. Even if it meant trusting Namaari.

"How would I even approach Namaari after all that's happened?"

"It may feel impossible. But sometimes you just have to take the first step, even before you're ready. Trust me," Sisu said.

Raya paused, looking at her ba. Finally, she agreed. "Okay. We'll go with your plan."

Sisu's face lit up. "What? My plan? You're gonna go with my plan?"

"Yeah," said Raya.

"All right!" Sisu swished her head with excitement. "You're not going to regret this. But we're going to need a really good gift. What do you think she's into?" She thought about it. "Cats? Knives? Cats with knives? Knives with little cats on them?"

"Actually," Raya interrupted. "I know exactly what to give her."

Reaching into her pocket, she withdrew the bronze Sisu pendant, the one Namaari had given her on the day they met. A gift from one dragon nerd to another.

Sisu beamed and nodded approvingly.

Raya climbed onto her back. As they rose into the sky, she glanced at her father one last time. Hopefully, the next time she returned to Heart, it would be to see him alive.

CHAPTER FIFTEEN

Namaari tore through the jungle of Fang's hinterland, urging her Serlot on. The cat's sides heaved with exhaustion. She knew it needed food and rest. But they couldn't stop now. In these wild regions, Druun attacks were common. Namaari knew it was only luck that had helped them avoid the Druun thus far.

After Raya's escape in the Spine village, Namaari and her army had turned immediately back toward Fang. Though her general had urged her to take a safer route, Namaari had chosen a risky shortcut. She was sure that Raya would turn up in Fang soon, looking for the Dragon Gem, and she wanted to be ready for her.

Namaari needed to speak with Chief Virana urgently. She now understood why Raya was collecting Gem pieces. With the Dragon Gem intact, Sisu could wipe away the

Druun, just as she had five hundred years before. Would Fang offer up their piece of the Gem to help?

The idea of helping their enemies went against everything Namaari had ever been taught. And yet . . .

As she raced along, Namaari replayed the moment with Sisu over and over in her mind. The dragon had looked right into her eyes, and Namaari had seen something that surprised and unsettled her. What was it?

Namaari was nearly to Fang before the answer came to her. Sisu had looked at her with compassion. And hope.

A soldier's cry broke Namaari's thoughts. The ground shuddered violently as three Druun suddenly rose from the earth behind them.

The Serlots leapt forward with newfound speed. With no protection, their only hope was to outrun the Druun.

In the near distance, Namaari saw the shimmer of water. The canal that separated Fang from the mainland was just ahead. If they could reach the water, they would be safe. Namaari leaned forward in the saddle. She could hear the Druun's ghastly hissing close behind. They seemed to be right on their heels.

The Serlots leapt off the edge of the canal, landing on the platform ferry that waited in the water. As Namaari and the soldiers pushed off, she looked back at the Druun.

They howled furiously, then disappeared back into the earth.

When the warriors arrived to the island of Fang, Namaari left the soldiers tending to the Serlots and hurried to the palace.

She found her mother in the courtyard. A small group of children from the village sat at her feet. Wide-eyed and open-mouthed, they listened as Chief Virana told them tales of the glorious history of Fang. Describing how their ancestors had outsmarted the Druun was one of the chief's favorite pastimes.

Usually, Namaari enjoyed her mother's little history lessons. But this time, she was in no mood to wait. When Chief Virana paused for breath, she interrupted. "Mother, we need to talk."

"It's Princess Namaari!" one of the kids cried. Several others cheered. Namaari smiled and bowed her head. To the children of Fang, she was a hero—the kind of warrior they all hoped to be one day.

Chief Virana stood. "All right, all right. Now run along, kittens," she said. "I have to speak with the princess."

Parents came in and ushered the children away. When they were alone, Namaari glanced up and said, "Mother, you won't believe what I saw—"

"You saw a dragon," Virana interrupted. Namaari was taken aback but kept her head lowered. "General Atitāya informed me that you'd be returning home without the Gem pieces," her mother said.

"It was Sisu," Namaari explained. "She can fix what we broke. She can bring everyone back."

"And that's what scares me," Virana replied. "When everyone comes back, who do you think they'll come for? You forget, the other lands blame us for what's happened."

"But we never meant for anyone to get hurt." Namaari thought her mother would be happy. But now she saw the deep crease between Virana's eyebrows.

"Yes, but if we had the dragon and the Gem pieces, we would be forgiven. We could save the world. More importantly, our people would remain safe."

"Raya isn't just going to give Sisu to us," Namaari said.

Virana sighed. "We're not going to give her a choice," she replied.

"What are you going to do?" Namaari was worried.

Virana stood and put her hands on Namaari's shoulders. "That's no longer your concern, my love. You've done enough." Then she turned and left with her general, leaving Namaari looking after them in alarm.

CHAPTER SIXTEEN

Raya and her friends stood on the bank of the canal. Together, they looked out across the water toward Fang. Against the blue twilight sky, Fang's palace looked like some sort of enormous bird of prey, its winged roofs seeming as if they were about to take flight.

As soon as it was dark, they would put their plan into action—bring the gift to Namaari and hope she would cooperate. But as the light drained from the sky, Raya's mind churned with doubt.

"If she refuses to help, we've just flushed our tactical advantage into the dung pot," Tong said. He'd been in a foul mood ever since Sisu and Raya returned from Heart. Raya knew it was because he didn't like Sisu's plan. He thought they were being foolish.

"I know," Raya said, her stomach twisting. *Trust,* she

reminded herself. She had promised Sisu that she would try.

But what if Sisu was wrong about Namaari? If so, they weren't just risking losing the Gem. They were putting their lives in danger.

"Yeah. She really has no reason to help us," Boun agreed.

"I know," Raya said again.

"This jerky is terrible," Sisu said, gnawing at a piece.

"I *KNOW*!" Raya exclaimed.

"Are you sure those four miniature menaces will be successful?" Tong asked Raya.

"I . . . don't know."

The sky was dark now. An almost-full moon shone down brightly on the canal, lighting a path toward Fang.

Raya turned to the Ongis and the con baby and nodded. It was time.

The baby and her furry friends slipped into the canal. They began to swim toward Fang. Raya watched uneasily as the four small heads moved away.

The plan was for the baby and the Ongis to sneak into the palace grounds and deliver the dragon pendant to Namaari, along with a note proposing their deal: one Dragon Gem piece in exchange for saving the world. Raya knew Namaari and the Fang army would be expecting her. But they wouldn't be on the lookout for a baby. The toddler and her furry friends had the best chance of slipping past the guards unnoticed. Having seen them in action in Talon, Raya felt sure they could handle it.

But as the time passed and the moon rose, Raya's confidence faltered. She imagined all the things that could go wrong. What if the baby was kidnapped? What if the Ongis were distracted by food and forgot their mission? What if they never even made it to Fang Palace? What if a current had already swept them away?

Raya paced on the bank, her mind spinning with worries. She had sent a toddler and three puny animals into enemy territory. What had she been thinking?

It had been hours since the baby and her friends had left. Raya had just decided to mount a rescue mission when she spied four small shapes swimming toward them. The con baby and the Ongis climbed, dripping, onto the bank. Raya could tell from the look on the baby's face that they'd done it.

They didn't know how long it would take for Namaari to come to them, and Sisu argued there was no point in waiting on an empty stomach. So the group returned to the Shrimporium for a last meal before whatever came next.

While Raya stood as a lookout, Tong and Boun argued

over the best way to make soup in the boat's makeshift kitchen.

"There's too much spice," Tong said, tasting the broth.

"Uh, no, there's too much bamboo," Boun countered.

Tong scowled. "What do you know? You have the taste buds of a tall baby."

"Well, you dress like a tall baby," Boun shot back.

"Give me the spoon! I'm taking over!"

Boun spun and dodged, holding the spoon out of Tong's reach. "Back off, tidal wave. I'm the professional here."

Laughing, Raya stepped in to break up the fight. "May I?" She pulled a pinch of palm sugar from her pouch and sprinkled it into the simmering pot.

Boun and Tong both tasted the broth and smiled. It was delicious!

"Whoa. That's good!" Boun said.

"It's just a little something my ba showed me."

"Aw. Did he also show you how to make that delicious jerky?" Sisu asked.

"No, that was all me. It'll be nice to share a meal with him again."

In addition to the hot soup, Boun and Tong had made rice, spring rolls, and a spicy salad of green fruit. Laid out on the table, it was a feast like Raya hadn't seen since she left Heart. Boun ladled the soup into bowls and handed them out.

Raya had eaten several bites before it dawned on her: she was eating food someone else had made. What's more, she was happy about it. She gazed around the table, surprised by the affection she felt toward her new friends. Their presence seemed to fill her with warmth as much as the hot soup did.

"I know what you mean," Boun said, interrupting her thoughts. "I have this really obnoxious sister who always tousles my hair. I can't wait to see her the most."

"After we win the day, I look forward to filling my eyeball with the joy-tastic image of my village full again," Tong said.

The baby, who was sitting on his shoulder, started babbling.

"And you will be reunited with your family, Noi," Tong told her.

Raya looked at him in surprise. "Um, what did you just call her?"

"Noi," Tong said matter-of-factly. "It's her name. It's written on her collar." He looked around the table in astonishment. "Have none of you ever checked?"

Raya, Sisu, and Boun all ducked their heads guiltily. Tong gave a grunt of disgust. "And they think of *me* as the ruffian," he murmured to Noi.

A firework exploded in the distance, above Fang. They all looked up to see the burst of red light.

"What's that mean?" Sisu wondered.

Raya stood up from the table. "It means we're on."

The others pushed back their bowls and rose, too. They began to collect their weapons.

"Sisu, until we get that Gem and confirm Namaari's actually on our side, promise you'll stay hidden," Raya said.

To Raya's relief, Sisu nodded. The dragon ducked into the forest. She watched through the trees as Raya hurried down to the water's edge.

Namaari was waiting for her. She held a cloth-wrapped bundle in her hands. For a moment, the two stared at each other.

"I see you got my gift," Raya began.

"I never thought I'd see this again," Namaari said, looking at the pendant.

"Well, I tried to take good care of it," Raya said.

Namaari looked up at Raya.

"You're not the only dragon nerd here," Raya added.

Namaari laughed. She looked at the cloth in her hands. Immediately, Raya could see the gleam of the blue-green shard. Without taking her eyes from Raya, Namaari placed the Gem piece on a rock between them and backed away.

At that moment, Sisu emerged from the woods, her eyes on Namaari. Namaari gasped and quickly bowed to her, then stood, looking a little shy.

"The final piece!" Sisu said to Raya.

"Time to bring everyone back," Raya said, and smiled.

Then she started to open her satchel, where the rest of the Gem shards sat, but she stopped when she heard a threatening *click*. She looked up, and her heart seemed to stop. Namaari held a raised crossbow. Her finger was on the trigger. Raya frowned and slowly put her hands up.

"Sisu and the Gem pieces are coming with me," Namaari said.

Behind them, the bushes rustled. Tong emerged from the forest. Boun, Noi, and the Ongis were right behind him.

"Sisu!" Boun yelled.

"Stay back!" Namaari warned.

Tong bared his teeth. "It was foolish to trust someone from Fang."

"Don't come any closer!" Namaari warned again.

Raya pleaded. "Namaari, it doesn't have to be like this."

Tears glittered in Namaari's eyes. But she didn't lower the weapon. "I don't have any other choice."

Raya's hand went to her sword.

"Hey. I got this," Sisu said softly. Raya paused, then slowly took her hand off her sword.

Sisu, starting to glow, took a few steps toward Namaari. Namaari now pointed her crossbow at Sisu.

But Sisu kept moving forward. "I know you don't want to hurt anybody."

"What are you doing?" Namaari asked.

"You just want a better world. Like we all do."

Namaari hesitated. She lowered her crossbow an inch. "Sisu . . ."

"I trust you, Namaari."

But Raya still wasn't so sure. She kept her eye on Namaari's trigger finger. Suddenly, it seemed to move. Raya didn't waste a moment. She pulled out her sword and rushed at Namaari.

But as she struck the crossbow, the trigger released. With a sound as quiet as the breeze, the arrow flew through the air and sank into Sisu's heart.

For one long, terrible moment, the world seemed to hold its breath. Raya, Namaari, and the others watched, frozen in horror, as Sisu tipped backward and plunged into the canal.

"No!" Raya screamed.

Namaari threw down her crossbow, grabbed her Gem piece, and took off.

Raya ran toward the water. "Sisu!" She could see the faint outline of Sisu below the surface. "No. . . ."

Tong, Boun, Tuk Tuk, Noi, and the Ongis all came to her side, but she hardly noticed. She was overcome with rage.

Abruptly, the water in the canal began to roil and sink, as if it was rapidly draining away.

"What's happening?" Boun cried. His eyes were wide with fear.

"I don't know. It appears that with the last dragon gone, so too goes the water," Tong replied. "Now there is nothing to stop the Druun. Nothing."

Across the newly empty riverbed, clouds of Druun emerged to overtake the city of Fang.

"Raya—" Boun said, then broke off. He looked around. "Where's Raya?"

On the ground lay the sheath of Raya's sword and the satchel holding three Gem pieces. Raya was gone.

CHAPTER SEVENTEEN

The city of Fang was in chaos. The ground shook and buildings crumbled as a storm of Druun swept through. Everywhere, people screamed and ran, trying to escape the swirling darkness.

As Raya climbed the steps of Fang Palace, people shoved past her, fleeing for their lives. Raya barely noticed their cries. The only sound she heard was the furious pounding of her own heart.

With her sword by her side, she strode right past the palace guards. None of them moved to stop her. They couldn't—they'd all been turned to stone.

A cloud of Druun swooped toward Raya. But when she raised her Gem shard, they shrank away, and she passed through unharmed.

Raya found Namaari in the throne room. She was

standing before a statue of her mother, Namaari's head bowed in grief. Even Chief Virana had not been safe from the Druun.

Thanks to Namaari, Raya thought, no one would ever be safe again.

"Namaari!" she cried.

The princess turned. When she saw Raya with her sword raised, Namaari's face hardened. "Let's finish this, binturi." She drew out two long knives.

As Namaari came toward her, Raya rushed forward with a roar. Her sword flashed through the air.

Namaari was the most skilled fighter Raya had ever met. And though she fought fiercely while Fang Palace started to crumble around them, her skill was no match for Raya's rage. Raya poured her fury and heartbreak into every blow. She struck for Sisu, for her ba, for the beautiful world that had been lost to them. . . .

With a swift blow, she knocked a knife from Namaari's hand.

Namaari lunged again. Raya countered, knocking her down. Namaari's other knife spun away across the floor. With a soft *plink,* the dragon pendant slid from her hands. Namaari scrambled to grab it. Raya stepped over Namaari, raising her sword.

Head bowed, Namaari clasped the pendant of Sisu to

her chest. "I never meant for any of this to happen," she gasped.

"Liar!" Raya roared.

"I don't care if you believe me," Namaari said. She kept her eyes on the pendant cupped in her hands. "Sisu did. But *you* didn't trust her. That's why we're here."

Raya hesitated. Every fiber of her being longed to strike Namaari down. But something held her back. Could what Namaari said be true? If she had only trusted Sisu, would the dragon still be alive?

"Do whatever you want, but you're as much to blame for Sisu's death as I am." Namaari closed her eyes, waiting for Raya's blow.

Raya caught sight of her own reflection in the blade of her sword. She was startled by the hatred she saw in her eyes.

She glanced back at Namaari. In one second, she could have her revenge. But was that the person she wanted to be? Was that what Sisu would have wanted? Or her ba?

A cry from outside penetrated Raya's thoughts. She glanced out the window and was stunned to see familiar faces.

When she'd left Tong, Boun, Tuk Tuk, and Noi in the woods, she'd left behind three of the Gem pieces to protect them from the Druun. But now they were here.

And they were using the pieces to help the citizens of Fang escape.

"Tong, there's still people back there!" Boun was yelling. "Hurry! We're running out of time."

"Got it! Everyone out! Come with me!" Tong cried, herding people before him.

Raya suddenly understood. She could help destroy the world, or she could help save it. That was the choice she had to make.

Leaving Namaari huddled on the floor, Raya ran to her friends.

Outside, the city was in chaos. Druun swarmed everywhere in an unrelenting whirlwind. Through the swirling clouds of darkness, Raya could faintly see the dim glow of her friends' Gem shards as they tried to fight the Druun off. She headed right toward them. She wanted to help however she could.

"Get to the water! Keep going! Keep going!" Boun yelled, brandishing his shard. Noi waved hers, too, managing to clear enough of a path for people to escape.

Tong was piling people onto his broad back. He raced them to safety, then returned for more. Even the Ongis were doing their part to keep the Druun away.

Raya helped load a group of terrified children onto Tuk Tuk's back. But each time she drove one Druun back, another swooped in. The Gem fragments were losing their power. The magic was dwindling.

"Okay, Tuk. These are the last of them," Raya shouted over the hissing growls of the Druun. "Go! We're right behind you!"

But as Tuk Tuk trundled off, a Druun rose up, blocking his path. The children on his back screamed.

"Tuk Tuk!" Raya rushed to help them. But the Druun was closer. It swooped hungrily toward her friend and the kids.

Suddenly, a lone figure leapt in front of Tuk Tuk, holding a glowing Gem piece high to drive back the Druun.

"What are you waiting for?" Namaari yelled at the startled Tuk Tuk. "Go!"

Raya gasped. Namaari turned toward Raya while Tuk Tuk hurried away with his cargo of children. But then, another earthquake hit. The ground beneath them cracked.

"Raya!" Boun shouted.

"It's the one who slayed Sisu!" Tong roared after he caught sight of Namaari.

The ground rolled again and gave way beneath their feet.

Raya felt herself falling down, down. Then the world collapsed around her, and everything went black.

CHAPTER EIGHTEEN

"**R**aya! Raya!"

Raya came to in darkness. Someone was calling her name. The sound seemed to be coming from far away.

She pushed herself up. The movement made her feel dizzy and sick. Her forehead throbbed. For a second, she struggled to understand what was happening.

With horror, Raya realized why it was so dark. The Druun had hemmed them in on every side, raging around them like a violent storm. Tong, Boun, Noi, and Namaari stood together with their backs to one another. They waved their Gem pieces, trying vainly to hold the monsters off.

Raya discovered her own Gem shard was still clutched in her fist. She staggered to her feet and joined them.

"The Gem's magic is almost gone!" cried Boun. The Gem pieces, once so bright, now had only a dull sheen.

Growling, Tong slashed his shard at a Druun, as if he was swinging his ax. The Druun shrank back, but only for a moment. Two more Druun advanced. "They aren't backing off!" he shouted.

"They're everywhere!" Boun exclaimed.

Raya heard a soft *plink* and looked down. The dragon pendant had fallen from Namaari's pocket. Raya leaned over and picked it up.

As she looked at the carving of Sisu, she had a flash of memory: she and Sisu standing together in the Chamber of the Dragon Gem. Sisu's words suddenly came back to her.

"I don't know why they chose me. It could have been any of us. All I know is I trusted them and they trusted me. And so . . ."

Raya's eyes opened wide. The answer had been there all along. Why had it taken her so long to see it?

"Everyone! Give me your gems!" she yelled over the roar of the Druun. "We can still put it together. It can still work!"

The others gaped at her as if she'd lost her mind. "Sisu's gone, Raya. We don't have her magic," Boun said.

"It's not about magic," Raya told him. "It's about trust."

"What?" Namaari asked.

"That's why it worked. That's why we can do it, too. By doing the one thing Sisu wanted us to do—what my ba wanted us to do—to finally trust each other and fix this. But we have to come together. Please."

"After what she's done?" Tong looked at Namaari in disgust.

"We'll never trust her!" Boun exclaimed.

Raya looked at her friends. She couldn't blame them. Only moments before, she had felt the same way.

"Then let me take the first step," she said. She went to Namaari and placed her Gem piece in Namaari's hand.

"Raya, no!" Boun cried. But it was too late.

The last thing Raya saw as the Druun swept over her was Namaari's pale face staring back at her in shock.

CHAPTER NINETEEN

Namaari clutched the Gem shard. She could still feel the faint warmth from Raya's hand in it, even as she watched Raya turn to stone.

When Namaari managed to tear her eyes away from Raya's frozen face, she found Tong, Boun, and Noi all staring at her. No one seemed to know what to do.

Boun looked at his Gem shard, looked at his friends, and then walked over to Namaari. Placing the Gem piece in her hand, he bowed and gave her a final glance.

As the Druun swept toward him, Boun took Raya's hand. When they'd finished with him, the boy's statue was huddled to her side like a child clinging to his mother.

Namaari felt something brush her leg. She looked down and saw Noi. The toddler was holding up her Gem piece, trying to give it to her.

Tong scooped Noi up. He added his shard to hers, then handed them both to Namaari, looking at her hard with his one eye. He cradled Noi in his arms as the Druun engulfed them.

The Ongis, rushing to stand around Tong's leg, were swept up, too. They all turned to stone.

Namaari had gotten what she wanted. All the pieces of the Dragon Gem—the last dragon magic in the world— were right here in her hands. She looked up and saw an exit.

She raised the Gem pieces, trying to drive the Druun back long enough to make her escape.

But as she did, her eyes fell again on the group of friends—and on Raya's face. Namaari saw something there she hadn't noticed before. Raya reminded her of Sisu. The first time Namaari had seen Sisu, the dragon had given her a look full of compassion. And hope. And trust.

Namaari dropped to her knees on the ground. Hurriedly, she tried to puzzle together the broken pieces. The glow inside each fragment was now no more than a faint glimmer.

Finally, she fit the pieces in place. At once, they fused together. The Dragon Gem was whole again.

Namaari placed a hand on Raya's shoulder as a Druun washed over her.

Moments later, the light within the Dragon Gem died.

CHAPTER TWENTY

The world went dark. For a moment, the only sound was the hissing of the Druun as they swept through the empty fields and buildings, searching for more souls to consume.

But then . . .

Deep within the Gem, there was a tiny flicker of light. Then it became a glow. The glow grew brighter and brighter and brighter . . .

BOOM!

White light exploded from the Dragon Gem. The ring of light radiated out, spreading to every corner of the lands. When it touched the Druun, they vanished instantly. In a single second, all the darkness was destroyed.

A deep silence followed. For the few people left alive to see it, the stillness was absolute. The world seemed to empty of any flicker of life. Even the wind had died.

Then, like a dragon awakening, thunder rumbled across the sky. Dark clouds gathered. And from them, a steady rain began to fall.

It fell on the broken buildings of Fang and on the silent, frozen villages of Spine. It fell on the windswept deserts of Tail and on the cramped marketplace in Talon. It filled dry, empty riverbeds all through Kumandra.

All over the lands, rain fell on the stone statues of the Druun's victims. As it did, the stone began to melt.

And the people came back to life.

Raya came to with a gasp, filling her lungs with a deep breath of air. A tingling warmth returned to her limbs.

She looked around, blinking in astonishment. She was alive. Truly and gloriously alive!

Raya felt a hand on her shoulder. With a start, she realized it belonged to Namaari. She watched as rain poured down on her former foe, turning her from stone to flesh.

Namaari awoke with a gasp. She met Raya's eyes, and they shared a look of understanding. Raya put her hand on Namaari's. Whatever had happened in the past, they were allies now. Next to them, Boun, Tong, Noi, and the Ongis were coming back, too.

"It worked! It worked!" Boun cried, trying to jump up and down on his frozen feet. He stumbled over them, tumbling to the ground. He wiggled his toes joyfully as the rain washed the last of the stone away.

Baby Noi squealed with delight as Tong swung her up into the air, laughing. Not wanting to be left out of the fun, the Ongis clambered up onto him, too.

Raya and her friends helped each other climb out of rubble.

Above, they found more wreckage. Huge sections of the palace had collapsed. The ground was a web of cracks. The Druun had destroyed so much.

And yet, it felt like a celebration. Everywhere she looked, Raya saw the people of Fang embracing loved ones they thought they'd lost for good. They danced and turned their faces to the sky as the rain poured down on them.

"Tuk Tuk!" Raya cried suddenly as her big friend rolled toward her. She laughed as they hugged, cheek to cheek.

A movement overhead drew Raya's attention. Something was coming toward them through the air. A crowd of bright, rippling shapes drew closer and closer.

The dragons had returned.

The colorful, majestic creatures soared overhead. They twisted and turned, running on raindrops as the people below stared up in wonder.

Raya felt a swell of joy and hope. It was the feeling she'd had watching Sisu fly the first time, but multiplied tenfold.

The dragons seemed to radiate peace, as if they embodied all the goodness in the world.

As one, the throng swooped toward the river. They hovered low over the surface and formed a ring. As they circled, the water began to glow and churn.

Suddenly, something in the shape of a ball rose up. It was Sisu, curled tightly, but starting to stretch. With a gasp, she blinked awake!

When she saw her siblings above her, the dragon's face lit up. "Pranee! Amba! Jagan! Pengu! Ha ha!" Sisu shouted as she climbed the raindrops to meet them and join their swirling formation.

After a long moment, Sisu broke away. She swooped down toward the island. Raya ran alongside her until, at last, she came to a stop.

"Raya," Sisu said, her voice full of pride.

Raya was so overcome with joy, she could only reply, "Sisu."

"I. Am. So hungry," Sisu said.

"I got some jerky," Raya joked.

Sisu smiled. "Not that hungry."

With great relief, Raya buried her face in the dragon's soft fur. She felt Sisu wrap her in a warm embrace.

"Soo-soo!" cried a little voice. They turned and saw Noi toddling toward them, her little arms outstretched. Tong,

Boun, and the Ongis were right behind her. Tong lifted Noi so she could grab the dragon's face in her favorite hug.

"Ah! It is good to breathe in your glorious dragon stench again," Tong said.

"Okay. I'll take that as a compliment," Sisu replied, looking past him.

They all turned. Namaari stood a few feet away, watching their reunion, her face a tangle of emotions. When she met Sisu's gaze, Namaari's eyes filled with tears. She ducked her head in shame.

Raya knew what she was thinking. Would the dragon ever forgive her for what she had done?

As if she could read her mind, Sisu swept out her tail. She pulled Namaari, Raya, and all their friends into a great big group hug.

CHAPTER TWENTY-ONE

The sun was just starting to rise when Tuk Tuk rolled to a stop on the Heart Bridge. Raya climbed down from the saddle. She took a deep breath, trying to steady her nerves. Her heart was jumping like a wild Ongi in her chest.

A lone figure stood on the bridge, looking lost. Raya watched silently as her father limped over to pick up a broken flag. As he looked at it, his shoulders slumped with sadness.

"Ba," Raya said softly.

Chief Benja turned. His mouth opened in surprise. The flag fell from his hands. "Dewdrop?"

With a sob, Raya ran into her father's arms. He hugged her tightly, stroking her hair.

Tears streamed down Raya's face. For so many years,

she'd dreamed of this moment. She almost couldn't believe it had finally come. She never wanted to let him go.

But after a moment, Benja stepped away. When Raya looked at him, she saw he was gazing past her, his face full of awe.

Without even turning, Raya knew why. He had spotted Sisu.

As the dragon stepped onto the bridge, Benja bowed to her in respect, forming his hands in a circle over his forehead. Raya bowed, too.

"Is that . . . really her?" Benja whispered to Raya, as if he didn't trust his own eyes.

Raya nodded.

"Chief Benja," Sisu said, her voice warm with affection. "Your daughter did you proud. I hope you don't mind . . . she brought some friends."

Sisu stepped aside. Benja looked past her, stunned.

A beaming Boun stood with his family. Noi waved from her mother's arms, as the Ongis sat on neighboring shoulders. Tong stood with his wife and baby and fellow Spine warriors. Namaari was there with Chief Virana. All of them bowed deeply.

And behind them, stretching far into the distance, were hundreds more people from Tail, Talon, Spine, and Fang, all standing side by side. Tears of joy filled Benja's eyes.

In pairs and groups, the multitude started to cross the bridge, each individual bowing to Chief Benja as they passed.

Raya smiled and squeezed her father's hand. "Ba," she said. "Welcome to Kumandra."